THE SURGEON'S
BABY SURPRISE

BY
CHARLOTTE HAWKES

MILLS &
BOON
™

First published in Great Britain 2017
By Mills & Boon, an imprint of HarperCollins*Publishers*
1 London Bridge Street, London, SE1 9GF

Large Print edition 2017

© 2017 Charlotte Hawkes

ISBN: 978-0-263-06708-8

Printed and bound in Great Britain
by CPI Antony Rowe, Chippenham, Wiltshire

33905541

Born and raised on the Wirral Peninsula, England, **Charlotte Hawkes** is mum to two intrepid boys who love her to play building block games with them and who object loudly to the amount of time she spends on the computer. When she isn't writing—or building with blocks—she is company director for a small Anglo/French construction company. Charlotte loves to hear from readers, and you can contact her at her website: charlottehawkes.com.

Books by Charlotte Hawkes

Mills & Boon Medical Romance

The Army Doc's Secret Wife

Visit the Author Profile page
at millsandboon.co.uk.

To my wonderful little boys, Monty & Bart.
I love you both *'to a million pieces'*—xxx

PROLOGUE

'DIFFICULT CASE, DR PARKER?'

Evie snapped her head off the cool glass of the vending machine at the unmistakeably masculine voice and tried to quash the fluttering of attraction suddenly tumbling in her stomach, despite her inner turmoil.

When was she going to get over this particularly inopportune attraction?

A moment ago, her brain had been swimming with a particularly challenging case. After a day of fighting for her patient and consistently hitting a brick wall, she was feeling drained and unhopeful, but a question from one of Silvertrees' foremost plastic and orthoplastic surgeons, Maximilian Van Berg, and she felt more fired up than ever.

Just as she did every time she was around the man.

Evie hastily dredged up a bright smile. Professional but not too flirty. He liked professional, as demonstrated by his use of her title rather than just using her first name as other colleagues did. And he didn't care much for flirts—any more than Evie cared to be thought of as one.

'Nothing I can't handle, Mr Van Berg.'

None of this *Dr* Van Berg for Max. He was old-school, trained by the Royal College of Surgeons, and he used his right to revert to *Mr* to reflect that.

'That I don't doubt,' Max murmured to her surprise before turning to the vending machine. 'Has this thing been swallowing money again?'

Wait, did he just compliment her—and in a voice that was sexy as hell?

Her nerve-endings tingled at the uncharacteristic gravelly tone. She was used to his clipped all-business tone with colleagues. In fact it was a shame Maximilian Van Berg wasn't a paediatric plastic surgeon—she got the feeling he wouldn't put his own reputation ahead of the best interests of a patient. He had attended the Youth Care Residential Centre where she normally worked a few times, and they'd always seen eye to eye on the cases then. Part of her itched to run this case by him, too, but he would certainly deem that unprofessional of her. She needed to push all thoughts from today out of her head for the night, think about other things and come back to it, refreshed, in the morning.

Instead, Evie allowed herself a covert assessment of the man beside her. He was wearing off-duty gear, which, she concluded grudgingly, only managed to underscore a muscled, athletic physique more suited to some chiselled movie star than the gifted surgeon the man actually was. As a psychiatrist, Evie only came to Silvertrees when she referred a case from her centre for troubled teens, but even she knew that Max was the golden boy of the hospital. And it hadn't surprised her to learn how high a proportion of the hospital staff had apparently attempted to land the man, succumbing to the heady combination of undeniable surgical skills and brooding good looks.

But it seemed that what made him most irresistible was the fact that Max was also intensely private. He was committed to his career, notoriously elusive, and inflexible in his rules about keeping emotions and personal life out of his department; on the rare occasions he was snapped by the media at high-profile events, his dates were always the most stunning media starlets, hanging perfectly on his arm. He strongly disapproved of co-workers dating and had even earned himself the moniker Demon of Discipline. She had never known him to break his own rules, and she could still hear the censure in his tone when he'd heard about her semi-relationship with one of his colleagues.

And yet, during her not infrequent visits to Silvertrees, hadn't she sensed some kind of spark between the two of them whenever they'd met?

Not that she meant to act on it, of course. She knew his rigid reputation only too well, which was one of the reasons she'd enthused about whatever—in reality, lacklustre—relationship she'd been in at the time they'd first met. And it had worked: Max had relaxed in her company, assured that she wasn't flirting with him. Still she'd sometimes felt there was an uncharacteristic softness from him during the rare moments they'd been alone together.

'Dr Parker?' He broke into her musings. 'I asked if the vending machine has been swallowing money again.'

Evie glanced through the glass panel to the item currently lodged, frustratingly precariously, on the half-open metal distribution arm, and sighed.

'The last of my small change…' she nodded, unable to help herself from adding '…and I'm starving.'

Evie tried not to gape as he fished in his pocket for coins for her. Or to notice the way his trousers pulled tantalisingly taut around well-honed thighs as he did so.

'What were you after?' he asked, his eyes not leaving hers.

Evie startled. If it had been anyone else offering to buy her a vending-machine snack she doubted she would have hesitated, but with Max it somehow seemed a more intimate gesture.

'It's just a granola bar, Dr Parker.' He sounded almost amused, as though he could read her thoughts.

She was being ridiculous; she gave an imperceptible shake of her head. It was foolish to allow her own futile attraction to him to lead her to imagine there was more to the simple act than he actually intended.

'As it happens,' she managed wryly, 'it was the raspberry and white chocolate muffin.'

'A sweet tooth.' He smiled. 'I didn't imagine that.'

A charge of heat fizzed through her. Logically, Evie knew he meant nothing by it but she couldn't shake the idea that he'd imagined anything about her at all. Just a shame it wasn't the same X-rated images she'd been unsuccessfully fighting whenever *she* imagined *him*.

'It's a weakness.' She fought to show a casual

smile, but she couldn't help her tongue from darting out to moisten suddenly parched lips.

As Max's eyes flicked straight down to the movement, Evie could have kicked herself for giving too much away. All she could do now was hold her ground and feign innocence, fighting the tingling heat as his eyes tracked up to meet hers. Boy, she hoped he couldn't really read her thoughts.

'Mine's dark chocolate,' he replied eventually, releasing her gaze as he turned flippantly back to the machine.

'Sorry?' She drew in a surreptitious deep breath.

'My weakness. At least seventy per cent cocoa solids, though probably not more than eighty-five.'

As weaknesses went it was hardly significant yet she felt a thrill of pleasure. In all the time she'd known him she'd never once known him to make such small talk. It loaned her an unexpected confidence.

'I didn't think the lauded Max Van Berg had any weaknesses,' she teased daringly.

'I have them.' He met her gaze head-on again. 'I just make it a point not to show them.'

She swallowed abruptly before taking the proffered muffin from him and promptly tearing off a chunk as her empty stomach growled its appreciation. It had been a long, busy day.

'I can't believe you're still here, going through patient files. Shouldn't you be home, sleeping after a long shift? Or is that another weakness in your book?'

It was meant to be a joke but in her nervousness it came out more clipped than she'd intended. Fortunately, he didn't seem to notice as he cast a grim gaze up the corridor.

'No, I was boxing off my open cases before I leave next week.'

'Oh, that's right.' Evie dipped her head; she remembered hearing something about that. 'You're going away to work with Médecins Sans Frontières, aren't you?'

'An eight-month project in the Gaza Strip,' he acknowledged grimly, shadows chasing across his handsome profile as he turned his head away. 'Helping burn victims, performing reconstructive surgery, amputations.'

'From the fighting?' Her heart flip-flopped at the idea of him risking his life in such an environment.

'Sometimes.' Max shrugged. 'But around seventy-five per cent of my patients will be kids under five years old.'

'I don't understand.'

'Electricity is cut off on a daily basis so the people rely on power from domestic-size gas containers for cooking or to heat their homes. But because the canisters are such poor quality, explosions are an everyday occurrence, and children are usually the victims.'

'It sounds like...rewarding work,' she managed weakly, studying his expression of grim determination.

'It is,' he agreed.

And it was essentially Max Van Berg. On the occasions she'd been to Silvertrees, Evie had found he was the surgeon every trauma doctor wanted to hear was on call for any orthoplastic cases with trauma victims from the A&E. She certainly wasn't surprised that MSF had snapped up a surgeon of Max's calibre.

'I wish every surgeon had your desire to help,' she murmured.

'Problems?'

Why was she hesitating? What did she have to lose?

'It that why you were leaning on the glass, staring so grimly into the machine when I first came into the lounge?' he enquired. 'Because it wasn't for your lost muffin.'

Evie wrinkled her nose. He moved to the coffee machine as she followed on autopilot, refusing to let him intimidate her and trying to ignore the defined muscles that bunched and shifted beneath his black tee shirt.

'I was just thinking about my patient,' she hedged.

'Go on.'

She smiled as his interest was instantly piqued. She could have taken a bet on that. Anything patient-related and it had Max's attention.

'Like I said, nothing I can't handle.'

'I imagine you can,' he repeated. 'We've worked together a couple of times now, Dr Parker. You're focused and you're dedicated to your patients but you don't make rash decisions. I respect your opinion as a psychiatrist, Doctor, and I like that.'

She stared at him in delight until the happiness turned to heat as he pinned her down with an intense gaze of his own.

'I like that a lot,' he repeated, his voice a low rumble. 'In plastics particularly, it's important to me to know who wants my help, and who truly needs it to turn their life around. Sometimes it's easy to tell but other times it isn't so clear-cut.'

Caught in his regard, she felt the atmosphere between them shift slightly. Heat began to rise in her face, travelling down her neck, through her chest until it pooled at the apex between her legs. This was the effect Max always had on her. Sometimes, the way he looked at her almost convinced her he was attracted to her, too.

But that was just fanciful thinking, wasn't it? She'd give anything to know what he was thinking, *right now.*

'Thank you, I—'

'So, how's she doing?'

'Sorry?'

'Your patient with the significant breast asymmetry.'

Another thrill fizzed through Evie. *Had he been watching her?*

She hastily reprimanded herself. It was the cases Max was interested in, not the fact that she was on them. She shouldn't be surprised that he knew the patient. She would bet he kept track of all the cases that came through his department—he was that kind of conscientious surgeon.

'That *is* why you were staring so distractedly into the vending machine, I take it? I also heard you've been reading the Riot Act to one of my colleagues. Are you always this passionate about your patients, Dr Parker?'

Evie blinked, suddenly thrown. His guess might be off, but his assessment of her state of mind was surprisingly on the money.

She had always got deeply involved with her

patients, it was true. Her work at the centre had always been more than a job; it had been a calling. But he was right, this case felt personal. She needed to win this battle and help this young girl change her life.

Because this week Evie had received the worst news of her life. Her own body was failing her and soon she might not even be able to help herself, let alone anybody else.

It hadn't been completely out of the blue. Fifteen years ago she'd been diagnosed with polycystic kidney disease, PKD, but she'd never shown any symptoms. However, during her routine check-up this week, to her shock, decreased kidney function had been detected. Her nephrologist had warned her that, whilst she could continue as normal for now, within the next six to twelve months she would begin to feel too exhausted to even continue as a doctor, and within a couple of years she would need a kidney transplant.

If she didn't get a new kidney she would never be able to help another troubled child, never have a child of her own. Worst-case scenario, she might not even have her life.

She hadn't confided it to a soul. She hadn't wanted to. And part of her had an inexplicable urge to spill all her fears to this man right here, right now. If she could trust anyone with this secret, it would be Maximilian Van Berg.

Yet another part of her held back. Better to stay away from her personal problems, concentrate on someone she *could* help: her patient.

Evie drew in a breath and sipped tentatively at the hot drink to steady her nerves.

'Honestly, it's just that my patient really does need this operation, not just for the obvious physical benefit but, as far as I'm concerned, for her mental well-being. She's on the brink of psychological depression, becoming more and more disruptive in school, and becoming so reclusive that her social skills aren't developing.'

'The issue, as I've seen, is that one of her breasts is barely an A-cup and the other is almost a D-cup, so the need for an operation in the future is inevitable?' he stated abruptly.

'Right.' Evie nodded as Max frowned. So he *had* been looking into the case file.

'She can't wear a bra that fits, she can't go swimming with her friends, or go to friends' houses for a sleepover. She can't even change in front of them for a basic PE lesson in school without being taunted. It's making her withdraw socially, and she's now developing stress-induced Irritable Bowel Syndrome.'

'I read the file, Dr Parker,' he responded, removing his drink from the machine and taking a generous gulp.

The man must have an asbestos mouth.

She gave an imperceptible shake of her head to refocus her thoughts.

'However, the paediatric surgeon we spoke to doesn't want to operate due to her young age. He doesn't want to operate when the patient is still growing and developing, and he doesn't know if she could cope mentally with the procedures, including an implant.'

'He has a point.'

'I appreciate that, and you must know how cautious I am about making such recommendations. But I've worked with this girl for almost a year. I don't believe its body dysmorphic disorder, and I know it's a fear of all paediatric plastic surgeons that they could miss such a diagnosis. In this case it clearly isn't an imagined or minor so-called defect in her appearance. It is something which is understandably imposing significant limitations on her life.'

'And what about realising the impact of these procedures? Does your patient understand that her body will never be perfect, that she will have to deal with the scars from the operation?'

'She absolutely does understand that. But, in her own words, the scar is something she could live with. It wouldn't prevent her from wearing a bra, or a swimsuit, or a prom dress. All things she currently can't do.'

He pinned her with a look that was more about the undercurrents running between them than the conversation they were ostensibly having.

'And your assessment is that this procedure isn't just about rectifying the physical problem but is necessary for developing well-being?'

'I think it's essential to her self-esteem and her social development at this crucial time in her life, Mr Van Berg.'

Her hands shook as she took another steadying sip of her coffee, her eyes still locked with his over the plastic rim.

'Then I'll take a look at the case before I leave.'

'You would do that for her?'

'I told you before, I respect you as one professional to another,' he growled. 'So, how's the boyfriend?'

Evie stiffened. As it happened her latest attempt at a boyfriend had resulted in being unceremoniously dumped when his mother had deemed her *not good enough* for her precious son, after Evie had revealed that she would never be able to give the woman the longed-for grandchild.

She hadn't loved the guy, but, still, it had been painful. It had hurt being told that she wasn't good enough, an echo of the hurt she'd felt when her father had walked out all those years ago.

But surely Max couldn't know about her pathetic love-life? She'd be a laughing stock. Hospital gossip was an unstoppable machine, everyone knew that, but, not working at Silvertrees permanently, she'd always convinced herself that she escaped the worst of it. Still, if people *did* know, then she couldn't afford to lie to Max now.

'Gone.'

She fought to affect nonchalance.

'Good. He didn't deserve you anyway,' Max murmured, his hand reaching slowly up to lower the cup from her lips.

'You didn't know him,' she protested mildly.

'I know if he lost you, he's a loser.'

Evie swallowed hard, unable to tear her eyes away from his.

'I'm going to check on your patient now. All I ask in return is that you join me for a drink in the bar across the way as soon as I can get away from this farewell party I'm supposed to be at right now.'

'What about your business and pleasure rule?' she whispered.

'In a few days, I won't even be in this country, let alone this hospital.' He gave a lopsided grin, so sexy it made her toes curl. 'I think we can bend the rules this once, don't you?'

His head inched closer until his nose skimmed hers. It was like some kind of exquisite torture.

She knew she should be strong, back away. But didn't she know only too well that life was short?

Stretching her neck, she closed the gap between them, a small sound of pleasure escaping her throat as her lips met his.

Max responded without hesitation. One hand slid around the back of her head as the other pulled her firmly to him. The reality of the feel of his solid body even more impressive than the eye had allowed the mind to imagine. His teeth grazed her lips as his tongue danced seductively. He might seem dedicated to his career and refuse to date within the hospital pool, but there was no doubting that Max had dated. He knew exactly what he was doing to her.

It was all Evie could do to raise her hands and grip his shoulders and she hung on for the ride.

'Is that you?'

'Is what me?' she muttered, frustrated that he'd pulled away from her.

'The beeper.' His voice was laced with amusement.

Slowly a familiar sound filtered into her head.

'Oh, that's me,' she gasped as her brain slowly clicked back into gear.

'Yes…' the corners of his lips twitched as she stood dazed and immobile '…Evangeline. You need to go now.'

'I do,' she murmured, muscle memory allowing her legs to start moving, backwards but in the right direction, even as her brain felt frazzled.

'I'll go and see your patient. When you're done with whatever your message is you can come and find me. I'll be back in my office.'

'I… Okay, I'll…see you later, Mr Van Berg.'

She watched Max turn smoothly and walk towards the double doors at the far end of the corridor, unable to stop him or say anything. It was only when her back slammed into something solid that she realised she'd reached the double doors at her own end.

She wanted to say something, but no words would come.

'Oh, and, Evangeline?' Max twisted his head to

call over his shoulder. 'For the rest of tonight shall we agree that it's *Max*, and not *Mr Van Berg*?'

A slow grin spread over her face as he disappeared through the doors.

CHAPTER ONE

EVIE PACED THE hospital corridor.

The wait was excruciating. The squeak of her shoes sounded unusually distracting as she slowly turned on the polished floor. The ever-present smell of disinfectant pervaded her olfactory senses in a way it never had before, so strong that she could almost taste it. Once she'd been a doctor here, now she was a patient like anyone else. She could wait in the visitors' room but there was already a woman in there who seemed to want to talk every time Evie was in there.

And anyway, out here she felt more in control, and closer to her sister-in-law, Annie. Beyond the double doors, Annie was going through yet another set of checks to confirm that she was still suitable to be Evie's living donor for a new kidney. But after almost a year and a bombardment of test after test to confirm compatibility and eligibility, these final cross-matching and blood-pressure checks still had to be run.

She subconsciously touched her lower abdomen, more out of habit than pain since the cramps had already subsided after today's dialysis session. Less than a week and this whole nightmare would hopefully be behind her.

Yet that wasn't even what had her heart performing its real show-stopping drum solo, as it had every single visit she'd made to Silvertrees since that night with Max, almost one year ago to the day. The double doors clanged at the end of the corridor, causing her to whirl around, her heart in her throat, just as it had been every other hospital visit in the last four months since he'd returned from Gaza. But it was always just patients or hospital staff she didn't know or barely recognised. Evie had no reason to think she would ever just *bump into* Max here. The transplant unit was in a dedicated wing set slightly apart from the main hospital. And yet every time she feared—and hoped—that the next person to walk through the doors would be him.

She could have chosen a different hospital, the one closer to where she now called home, but Evie's referral to the state-of-the-art facility at Silvertrees was like gold dust and she'd have been a fool to turn it down for fear of bumping into a man who, for all intents and purposes, had been nothing more than a one—okay, five—night stand.

At least, that was the argument she told herself, and the one she was sticking with. After the two catastrophic attempts she'd made to contact him when he'd still been in Gaza, to tell him about the baby they had created together, she wasn't about to admit out loud that some traitorous part of her secretly dreamed that Fate might intervene. That, in the silence of the night, a tiny, muffled voice challenged her to venture into the main hospital and find him.

Not that she had any idea what she would say to him. How she would even attempt to begin to explain the choices that she'd made. In her heart she knew everything she'd done had been for their baby—a miracle, given the deterioration in Evie's kidney condition at the time of the pregnancy—but it didn't make her feel good about herself.

And still.

She'd hardly been in a state to think clearly when she'd accepted the hush money. In a daze from her premature baby and her kidney failure, rushing between NICU and her dialysis sessions. So when Max's parents—the people who should have their son's best interests at heart—had told her that neither they, nor their son, would want anything to do with the baby, a fiercely protective new-mother instinct of her own had kicked in. She'd worked with enough troubled teens to know how damaging it could be when a child was unloved, unwanted. And she had her own painful experience of being left by her father, too.

Both she and Imogen deserved better than that. They deserved to be cherished, not made to feel like a burden. And so Evie had allowed herself to be persuaded it was in her precious baby's best interests not to tell Max Van Berg he was a father.

But what if she'd been wrong? What if Max *would* have wanted to know about his daughter? Her head whirled with doubts, drowning out the sound of the double doors slamming open once again.

'Evie?'

Goosebumps swept across her skin. She didn't turn around; she couldn't. The voice was painfully familiar and intensely masculine. It evoked a host of memories that Evie had spent a year trying unsuccessfully to bury. A prong of doubt speared her insides. Had she been wrong to believe he didn't care? Because in that perfect moment Max actually sounded happy—albeit a little shocked—to see her.

She swallowed ineffectually, her mouth too

parched, and her heart wasn't so much beating in her chest as assaulting her chest wall. Whatever she'd imagined, she wasn't mentally prepared for this but there was nothing else for it.

Steeling herself against the kick from the moment she laid eyes on Max again, Evie lifted her head boldly and completed a slow one-eighty.

She hadn't steeled herself enough.

'Max.' She gritted her teeth, striving to sound calm. In control.

'What are you doing here, Evie?'

There was still no trace of chilliness in his tone. *Was that a good thing, or a bad one?* It suggested he knew nothing about Imogen, so maybe there was still hope. But then again, it also meant he'd been happy with their fling and certainly hadn't been thinking about her these last twelve months so the bombshell of a daughter wouldn't be well received.

So she stayed silent and contented herself with drinking in the man she recalled so very intimately.

Time apart had done little to diminish the sheer physical presence he exuded and she was grateful for the few feet of space between them, acting as something of a safety buffer, both mentally and physically. But space couldn't erase everything. The way Max looked and the authority he exuded.

The feel of his skin beneath her hands and her body. The way he smelled—no overpowering aftershave for Max, but instead a faint, intoxicating masculine scent underpinned with a hint of lime basil shower gel she remembered only too well.

'Are you working here again?' he pushed.

'No.'

Silence hung between them.

'Evangeline, why are you here?'

She had to say something. She was standing in the middle of a dedicated transplant unit—she had to explain her visit somehow. So she settled for a half-truth.

'My sister-in-law has some tests before her appointment with Mrs Goodwin,' Evie started carefully, studying his face for any kind of reaction.

'Arabella Goodwin?' He frowned. 'The nephrologist?'

'That's right,' she confirmed slowly.

'Is it serious?'

Evie searched his face; she needed to be careful here. Really be sure of herself before she said anything.

Admittedly, he seemed genuinely interested, but that meant nothing. This was the side of Max she knew, his sincere concern for his patients and their families. But it didn't mean he wanted a family of his own. It just meant he was dedicated to his career.

Just as his parents had cruelly reminded her.

Just as they'd made her see that, for Max at least, their short-lived fling had been just that. It certainly hadn't been the start of something. He hadn't asked her to wait for him whilst he was away in Gaza. He hadn't even told her that his parents were the renowned surgeons she had read about, attended guest speaker talks to see, studied, throughout her medical studies.

In short, they had shared five nights and four days of intense, unparalleled intimacy, yet told each other so very little about their lives beyond the bedroom.

What if she told him everything now only for him—out of some ill-considered knee-jerk sense of obligation—to involve himself in their lives, only to resent his daughter's existence every time it even threatened to impact on his career?

Wasn't that the nightmare scenario his parents had painted for her? Right before they'd offered her enough money to secure her daughter's financial future in the event that her kidney transplant failed and she wasn't around to look after her precious daughter herself?

But it wasn't just what they'd said, it had been

their calm, assured delivery. As if they were acting in her interests as much as in their son's. As if they really believed that her taking the money and staying away was the best solution for everyone. *That* was what had convinced her to take their word for it.

The savage protectiveness Evie felt for her new daughter still caught her unawares sometimes. There was nothing she wouldn't do to protect her beautiful daughter from anything which—or anyone who—could potentially hurt her.

If the Van Bergs had been cruel or vindictive, she probably wouldn't have believed them, wouldn't have taken the money. But she'd been frightened. And vulnerable. Between her bleak prognosis and her premature baby, she hadn't been able to face a battle on a third front. And if his parents were right and Max didn't want to know, how could she face yet more anguish? She couldn't risk it. So now, she needed to buy herself time to think. She'd never expected to see Max again.

But was that completely true? Hadn't she always hoped, deep down, when she was stronger, and if the transplant was successful, that she might be able to track him down again? Hadn't she told herself that, if all went well, she would push past her own fears of rejection and loss to finally tell him about his daughter? For Imogen's sake, because her precious daughter deserved so much more.

But now was not that moment.

'Annie's going through final checks for a kidney transplant. Blood pressure and all that,' Evie trotted out.

She sounded more blasé than she'd have liked, but it was better than having to tell him Annie was actually a kidney donor and that she herself was the recipient. And it was better than breaking down and telling him how frightened she was.

She should have known better than to think she could fool someone as astute as Max. Disbelieving eyes raked over her and she tried to suppress the wave of heat at his intense assessment, all too conscious of the toll her illness and the pregnancy had taken on her over the last year. Dark pits circled her eyes, her frame was unattractively thinner, and her skin flat and pallid—no matter how much she tried to lift it with clever make-up.

She squirmed under his sharp gaze.

'God, Evie, I'm so sorry. I had no idea.' The reserved tone was gone again, replaced by an open candour she thought was more *Max-like*. 'Didn't you say you were close to your brother and his wife? No wonder you look so pale—you must be so worried about her.'

Her stomach flip-flopped. He'd actually remembered some of the few things she'd told him. Was that really something he'd have bothered to take notice of if it had *only* been about the sex? Her mind swirled with conflicting thoughts.

She jumped as she closed the gap between them, his hands closing firmly around her shoulders, drawing her in so that she had no choice but to look him in the eye.

'Evie, if you need anything, you know you can come to me, don't you?'

Residual sexual attraction still fizzled between them.

Chemistry. It's just chemistry, Evie repeated to herself, clinging to the mantra like some kind of virtual life raft. But her grip was slipping and a flare of hope flickered into life deep in her chest. At this stage of her renal failure, a man who could make her feel attractive, wanted, who could make her forget her constantly exhausted body and her regular rounds of dialysis, was a rare male indeed.

Only Max could have snuck under her skin in five minutes flat.

She so desperately wanted to let him kiss her, take her, reassure her that she was still a sexy, desirable woman. It would be welcome relief after the year she'd had.

But this wasn't about her, this was about Imogen, too, and Evie couldn't risk her daughter being drawn into some game as a pawn. Hadn't her own biological father used herself and her brother to hurt their mother? First by walking out on them when Evie had been a baby, with no contact for years, and then by trying to play them off against each other when their mother had finally found happiness with a new man. A kind man who Evie considered to be her true father rather than simply her stepfather. A man who had saved her from going down the kind of route that too many of her troubled teens now found themselves stuck on.

Even now, eighteen months on from the fatal car crash on the winding, twisting Pyrenees' roads on what had been her parents' second honeymoon to celebrate their twenty-fifth wedding anniversary, she still missed them.

It was the kind of close, loving relationship she'd always imagined for herself. The kind of relationship Max had never offered—could never offer—her.

She looked up into his dark eyes and shuddered.

Despite all her self-recriminations, the need to give herself up to Max, to take him up on his offer of support and to give in to her body's welcome burst of energy and unexpected ache for him, was all too thrilling.

'Here, put this on.'

It was only as Max was wrapping his coat around her shoulders that Evie realised he'd thought she'd shivered with the cold. She couldn't help casting a glance up and down the corridor, spotting a couple of nurses at the far end. Too far away to hear their words but watching their exchange with interest.

'Max, please,' she whispered. 'We're being observed.'

He followed her gaze to their curious audience and, muttering a low curse under his breath, turned her around and propelled them down the corridor.

'In here,' he ground out as he bundled her into an unoccupied room off the corridor. And so help her, she let him.

'What's going on, Evie?'

It took everything in Max to push her away from him when all he wanted to do was pull her into his arms and remind himself of her taste, her touch, her scent.

'I don't know what you mean.'

She was lying.

He'd spent the last year unable to get this singularly gentle, funny, sinfully sexy woman out of his head. So much for telling himself, before giving into temptation with her that night, that it would be a one-time fling. He'd always been a firm believer in avoiding dating workplace colleagues, something he'd had no problem adhering to before Evangeline Parker had come along. He wasn't exactly short of willing dates with women who had nothing to do with the hospital, or even the medical profession at all, yet no one had ever got under his skin as Evie had.

She was the first person to ever make him think about anything other than his career as a surgeon. To ever make him wonder if there was more out there for him than just reaching the very pinnacle of his speciality. It had only been that phone call from his parents, on the last evening of his time with Evie, that had unwittingly brought him back to earth.

They were skilled surgeons but cold, selfish parents, and his childhood had been bleak and lonely, a time he rarely cared to look back on. Talking to them that night had reminded him why he would not put any wife, any family, through the only home life he had known. It was a choice. Be a pioneering surgeon, or be a good family man. Never both.

And he could imagine that a family was what Evie would want. What she would deserve.

So he'd thrown himself into his eight-month tour in Gaza, appreciating the challenging working conditions, the difference he was making—and the fact that it was providing a welcome distraction from memories of that one wanton, wild, yet exquisitely feminine woman. However many amazing, lifesaving surgeries he'd performed, he'd always gone back to his tent at night wishing he could share the day's events with Evie. Wishing he were sliding into his emperor-sized bed with her rather than dropping onto his tiny cot, alone.

Yet now she was standing here in front of him, and he wanted her as much as he ever had, telling himself that the only reason he hadn't walked away from her was because she clearly needed someone to talk to. A flimsy excuse, since she clearly wasn't jumping at the chance of opening up to him. Just as they'd revelled in the sex but both been so careful to avoid much personal conversation those five hot-as-hell nights together.

'I think you do know,' he contradicted quietly. 'This is about more than just your sister-in-law and her kidney transplant, isn't it?'

Evie bit her lip, refusing to meet his eye.

'What do you mean?'

She didn't want to talk. But she probably needed to.

'You're concerned for her, frightened for her? That's understandable. But I'm guessing this is more about you feeling as though you need to be the strong one because you're the doctor, and people are looking to you for the answers.'

She chanced a glance at him but didn't answer, so he pushed on.

'It's very different being on the other side of the fence when you're used to being the one making the decisions, but I'm guessing you can't talk to Annie, or your brother, about your fears. So I'm offering for you to talk to me instead.'

'Why would you do that?'

She sounded bewildered. *Was he really that unapproachable?*

'Because I once told you I respect you as one professional to another.'

'I see.'

Was that a flash of disappointment? She shook her head, the moment gone.

'I can't.'

If he simply walked away then he'd feel like a cad. But if he pushed her then he risked misleading her into thinking that he was open to something more between them.

'Can't, or won't?'

She opened her mouth, closed it, and then opened it again.

'Can't. I want to, Max, more than you know. But I can't.'

There was no reason for his chest to constrict at her words. Yet it did. He gritted his teeth. As long as he could persuade her that there was nothing more between them—that he wasn't remembering how incredible it had been to undress her, lay her on the bed and kiss her until she came undone at his every touch—then she might talk to him. And she definitely needed to talk to somebody.

'Fine, let's discuss the elephant in the room.'

She swallowed hard.

'So, we had a one-night stand—'

'Five nights,' she interrupted, flushing bright red.

He felt a kick of pleasure. *So it mattered to her?*

'Okay, five nights,' he conceded, allowing himself a lopsided grin and watching her carefully. 'Five nights of, frankly, mind-blowing sex.'

She flushed again, crossing her arms over her chest as if to reinforce an invisible barrier between them. But it was too late—he'd seen the way her pupils dilated in pleasure at his words. She might not want to talk to him, but she was certainly still attracted to him.

Her breathing was slightly more rapid, shallower than before, the movement snagging his eye to the satin-soft skin his fingers recalled even now. Her lips parted oh-so-slightly as her tongue flicked out to leave a sheen glistening on her lips. An action that he'd experienced in other ways over those five nights. An age-old response had his body growing taut.

He needed to walk away.

He couldn't.

He closed the gap between them until he could feel her breath on his skin, smell that mandarin shampoo of hers in his nostrils.

'It doesn't have to be over,' he muttered hoarsely. 'Neither of us have the time or inclination for wasting time playing at relationships. But we're both consenting adults, why not enjoy the sex?'

'Just sex?' she whispered again.

He couldn't help it. Before he could stop himself, he reached his hand out and slid his fingers under her chin to tilt her head up. Her eyes finally met his and the sensation was like an electric shock through his body.

'Just sex,' he ground out, as much to remind himself as to convince her.

For a moment he thought she was going to turn him down, but suddenly she raised her hand to catch his and held it against her cheek. Closing her eyes, she rested her chin in his palm as though drawing strength.

'Evie.' His other hand laced through her silky hair to draw her to him; he inhaled her gentle scent, so painfully familiar. The feel of her hands gripping his shoulders then running down his upper arms, the way her breasts brushed against his chest, heating him even through the material that separated them both.

And then his mouth was on hers and Max couldn't be sure which one of them had closed the gap first. He didn't really care. With one hand still threaded through her hair, he trailed the other hand down her cheek, her neck, her chest, feeling her arch her back to push her breast into his palm.

He heard his low growl of anticipation as the hard nipple grazed his palm through the layers of thin cotton, dropping his hand so that he could flick his thumb across it. He dropped down to perch on the corner of the table as she moved over him and his thigh wedged between her legs, which pressed against him so that he could feel the heat at their apex. He dropped his other hand down her back to cup her wonderfully rounded backside, smaller than he recalled. And then she kissed him intensely and it was just the two of them as everything else fell away.

'God, I want you,' he groaned.

'How much?' she whispered.

'You must know the answer to that,' he rasped out, her uncertainty surprising him. The woman he'd known last year hadn't needed validation or reassurance, she'd been sexily confident in her own skin. Still, if she wanted him to show her then he was more than willing to oblige.

But before he could act, Evie had tugged his shirt out, the buttons opening easily beneath those nimble fingers of hers. Dipping her head, she nipped and kissed his body that was leaner and tighter than ever. It ought to be—he'd been hitting his home gym hard ever since his return from Gaza, the only way he could burn off excess energy since he hadn't wanted to sleep with any other woman since Evie.

As she made her way back up to his lips Max pulled her back into him, his hands sliding under the fitted blouse that followed the curves of her pert breasts, revelling in the way her breath caught in her throat.

Suddenly he froze. Her once slender form felt thin. Too thin. He could actually count her ribs. He drew back shaking his head; nothing was as clear or sharp as usual. *Was he missing something?*

'Evie, stop...'

And then Max felt her slump slightly, as though the sudden flame of energy she'd had had just been stamped out without warning.

He was a first-class jerk. Evie was worried about her sister-in-law and he was only interested in re-kindling the connection between them.

'I'm sorry, that should never have happened.'

Evie shook her head, and as she pulled away from him he clenched his fists by his sides just so that he didn't pull her back.

'No, it was my fault, Max.' She sounded distraught. 'I shouldn't have come back here.'

For the first time, Max wondered if he'd made a mistake. It wasn't a feeling he was accustomed to. He could read charts, he could read patients, he could read histories. He'd never been bothered to learn to read relationship signals before.

Dammit. Had he got it all wrong?

'Evie, is there something else going on here?'

'Leave it, Max. Please.' She stepped back so abruptly that she almost fell, but it was the pleading in her eyes that stayed his arms from catching her.

Max watched some inner battle war across her features, then, apparently unable to trust herself to say another word, she straightened up and forced her legs to move. He knew it wasn't the moment to stop her. He had some investigating to do before he charged in there.

He forced himself to stay still as she stumbled out of the room, the slamming door reverberating with raw finality.

CHAPTER TWO

IT WAS TIME for answers.

Max pulled up outside the unfamiliar house and turned the purring engine off with satisfaction. His sleek, expensive supercar—one of his very few real indulgences to himself—was incongruous against the older family cars and the backdrop of the suburban street. He checked the address he'd hastily scribbled down on the back of a hospital memo.

It was definitely the right place. But the nondescript, nineteen-fifties semi-detached house on a prepossessing street, almost ninety minutes from Silvertrees, was the last place he would have expected to find Evie—it all seemed so far removed from the contemporary flat that he was aware had come as part of her package working at the Youth Care Residential Centre.

But then, what did he know about the real Evie Parker?

And for that matter, what was he even doing here?

Instinct.

Because decades as a surgeon had taught him to follow his gut. And right now, as far as Evie was concerned, he couldn't shake the feeling that there was something fundamental he was missing. Sliding out of the car, he crossed the street, his long stride easily covering the ranging pathway from the pavement to the porch. He knocked loudly on the timber door, hearing the bustle on the other side almost immediately, before it was hauled open.

'Max.'

'Evangeline.' He gave a curt nod in the face of her utter shock, wishing he didn't immediately notice how beautiful she was.

And how exhausted she looked. He'd seen the dark rings circling her eyes yesterday, along with the slightly sallow skin, so unlike the fresh-faced Evie he'd known a year ago. Just like how thin she'd become, all clear indicators of the toll her illness was taking on her body. He could scarcely believe his surgeon's mind had allowed her to fob it off on being concerned for the health of her sister-in-law. But as soon as she'd gone and his gut had kicked back in, it hadn't taken much digging to discover that it was Evie who was unwell, not

Annie. That it was Evie who needed the transplant, not Annie.

He felt a kick of empathy. And something else he didn't care to identify. He shoved it aside; he was here to satisfy himself there really *wasn't* something he was missing, and to be a medical shoulder to cry on. Nothing more than that.

Evie stepped onto the porch, pulling the door to behind her, clearly not about to invite him in.

'What are you even doing here?'

Ironic that he had asked her the same question less than twenty-four hours earlier.

'Why did you tell me Annie was the one who needed the transplant?' He was surprised at how difficult it was to keep his tone even and level with her, when at work his professional voice was second nature.

Evie's face fell. He didn't miss the way her knuckles went white as she gripped the solid-wood door tighter.

'I didn't.' She tilted her chin defiantly.

'You implied it, then. It's semantics, Evie.'

'How did you find out?'

'I was concerned. Things didn't seem to add up.'

To her credit, she straightened her shoulders and met his glare with a defiant one of her own. *That* was the Evie he knew.

'You've been checking up on me? Reading my file?'

'You left me with little choice.' He shrugged, not about to apologise. 'And don't talk to me about ethics—for the first time in my career I don't care. You should have been the one to tell me, Evie.'

'Well, you should be sorry,' she challenged, although he didn't miss the way her eyes darted nervously about. 'You were the one who always used to be such a stickler about doctor-patient confidentiality.'

'Is this really the conversation you want to have?' Max asked quietly.

She stared at him, blinking hard but unspeaking. *One beat. Another.*

'You're right, I'm sorry,' she capitulated unexpectedly. 'Yesterday…it's been playing in my head and now I'm glad you know. I…just didn't know how to tell you.'

His entire body prickled uneasily.

'Are you going to invite me in?'

She fidgeted, her eyes cast somewhere over his shoulder, unable to meet his eye.

'First tell me exactly what you gleaned from my file?'

Max hesitated. There was something behind that question that was both unexpected and disconcerting. The Evie he'd known was feisty, passionate, strong, so unlike the nervous woman standing in front of him, acting as though she had something to hide, as much as she tried to disguise it.

'As it happens, I didn't read your file. You can relax. I just spoke to Arabella.'

'Sorry?'

'Arabella Goodwin, your nephrologist,' Max clarified patiently. 'I told her you'd approached me about the kidney transplant yesterday whilst your sister-in-law was having her tests done. Which, technically, you had done. Imagine my shock when she assumed I knew that Annie was a living donor and that you were the recipient.'

He'd just about managed to cover up his misstep with his fellow surgeon in time.

'Oh,' Evie managed weakly. 'What else did she say?'

'That your sister-in-law was in for the final repeat tests to ensure nothing had changed before the operation could proceed. I understand you're due for your transplant next week but you'll be taken in for the pre-op stage in a matter of days.'

'And?' she prompted nervously.

He frowned at her increasing agitation.

'Do you mean your PRA results and your plasmapheresis?'

He heard her intake of breath before she offered a stiff nod. His frown deepened. Her tenseness made no sense—surely she had to know that the Panel Reactive Antibody blood tests were undertaken by every potential renal transplant patient in order to establish how easy—or difficult—it would be to find a compatible donor?

What was he missing here?

'Evie, it isn't uncommon,' he tried to reassure her. 'You must know that around twenty-five per cent of patients who need renal transplants go through plasmapheresis to remove dangerous antibodies from their blood and increase their compatibility. You've nothing to worry about.'

'Did she tell you anything else about it?'

She asked the question quietly, but he didn't miss the shallow rise and fall of her chest.

'Evie, is this about your previous transplant not working? Is that why you're so frightened?'

'My previous transplant?'

He bit back his frustration at her resistance to confiding in him.

'You have high antibody levels, Evie, so either you've had a transfusion, a pregnancy, or a previous transplant. I'm guessing it's the latter, presumably when you were a kid?'

It would certainly explain her ever-increasing

agitation, if she was afraid her body would reject another kidney.

'You're guessing a previous transplant,' she repeated, almost to herself before twisting her head up to him again. 'You really didn't read my file.'

'Of course not.' Max blew out a breath. 'Although I admit I *was* tempted. But I didn't want to do that to you, or to a colleague like Arabella. I *do* want to hear it from you, though. Like I said last night, I can imagine you're having to be strong for your family and that leaves no one to be there to support *you*.'

Not least since, over the last twelve months, there must have been a veritable battery of tests for Evie. And for Annie, too. But it was Evie who concerned him, right now.

'Since when do you have the time to leave your surgeries?' she asked sadly. 'Or, for that matter, the inclination?'

It was a valid question. He didn't think he'd have even delayed a surgery for a five-minute coffee with a needy colleague in the past, let alone shuffle his schedule so he could drive a three-hour round trip, not to mention the fact that he was determined not to leave here until Evie had confided all her fears and uncertainties.

He wanted to help her. Needed to help her. There was no point pretending otherwise.

'Since it was you,' he answered honestly, 'I *made* the time.'

He'd sensed she needed the shoulder to cry on from the moment he'd run into her the previous day, but he'd had no idea just how much until she stared at him with wide, suddenly glistening eyes, before almost buckling at the door. He moved forward and swept her up before she hit the ground.

'Let's get you inside.'

He had no idea what Evie wanted from him as he carried her through the hallway. She was staring at him, blinking back the tears, and he felt as though she was evaluating him, as though somehow he'd just passed some kind of test he hadn't even realised he was taking.

He crossed over an original-looking, slightly broken-up parquet floor, past family pictures of people he didn't recognise, and past a coat rack sagging under the weight of coats and waterproof jackets in a rainbow of colours. Pairs of shoes and trainers, women's, men's and clearly a young boy's. An old pram and a box of toys.

There was no doubt it was a family house, practically bursting at the seams. And there was nothing of Evie he really recognised about it.

Finally reaching a quiet living room, just as packed with paraphernalia as the hallway, Max lowered her carefully to the floor.

'This isn't where I'd have pictured you. I take it this is your sister-in-law's home?'

'Yes,' Evie answered slowly. 'And my brother's, obviously. I lost my flat at the centre when I became too tired to work there. Annie invited me to move in with them about nine months ago when I…I needed the help.'

She stopped short of whatever she'd been about to say. He didn't think now was the time to push her.

'That can't have been an easy thing to do.'

'It wasn't,' Evie answered, her voice brittle.

'You sound surprised.'

'I didn't expect you to be so sympathetic. I thought you were all about career, career, career.' She chopped her hand in the air to emphasise her words. 'Drink?'

The sudden change of topic caught him off guard. Did she really think him so heartless?

'Okay.'

She left the room and he heard her bustle about the kitchen. He'd wanted to ask her what yesterday had been about, the way she'd kissed him, their intimacy. Had he pushed her, or was her desire for him genuine? But then, how could it be when she was as ill as she was?

Now didn't feel like the right moment to challenge her; he needed to bide his time. Standing up, Max searched for a distraction, for the first time allowing himself to look properly at their surroundings. A picture on the back wall caught his interest. A photo of Evie with what had to be her brother and sister-in-law at their wedding. His eyes scanned over the other photos, mainly of Annie's family, older ones of a baby, growing into a young boy maybe nine or ten years old. A couple with Evie in them, in various fashions and hairstyles, and Max smiled. There was no denying that Evie and her brother were siblings, with similar features and colouring, and yet, whilst Evie was undeniably feminine, her brother looked strong and confident. Not as if Evie needed Max to support her at all.

It should please him to think that Evie didn't need more help, yet Max found himself bridling at the idea that she didn't need him. Suddenly a baby photo on the bookshelf snagged his gaze.

Recent. Presumably the baby who used that pram in the hallway. The picture was in a double frame with one as the close-up of the baby that had first caught his attention, the other a photo of Evie with a new baby. A new niece most likely. The baby had to take after her father, but the similarities he'd already observed meant that he could imagine it would be what any baby of Evie herself could look like. Max's chest actually constricted. Evie looked particularly ill and yet the look of unadulterated love on her face was unmistakeable. He'd been right thinking this was exactly the kind of life, of family, that Evie would want for herself. The only reason she hadn't got it yet was because of her illness.

He could never give Evie the family she would want, once she got the transplant she needed. And it was foolhardy pretending he was here just for support for a woman who was, effectively, nothing more than a one-night stand. He needed to go. Get back to his life at Silvertrees. Refocus on his work. Forget about Evangeline Parker.

Moving quickly away from the photos and back to the armchair to wait for Evie, Max sought a way to best extricate himself. He'd have the drink she was preparing, and then make his exit.

'Anyway, I just thought I'd make sure you're okay. It's great that you have a living donor in your sister-in-law,' he offered when she came back through the door at last, a jug of orange juice and two glasses in hand.

'Yes.'

'No waiting on a transplant list. The procedure can be done at the earliest opportunity, before the body goes into kidney failure, and before it puts additional stress on your other organs.'

'Yes.'

He tried to bite his tongue as she poured the first juice, but as her hand hovered over the second glass, he couldn't stay silent.

'Are you supposed to be drinking that? I'd have thought you should be limiting your potassium intake.'

'What are you? The juice police?' she grumbled, but he noted that she set the jug down without pouring a glass for herself. Settling herself on the couch opposite him. Distancing herself once again.

'Evie...' his voice was gravelly with concern, startling even himself '...I'm here. Talk to me.'

So much for extricating himself.

Evie had barely managed to stop herself from sinking back into his arms and confessing everything. He was here.

Here.

And more than that, he'd uttered the words she'd never even dreamed she would hear from him. He had *made* the time to come to her because he knew she needed him.

He just didn't know how much, or why. And she had to be sure—she owed it to Imogen. She couldn't bring Max into her daughter's life until she knew it was absolutely worth it. That Max was worth it.

Not that she had a clue how she would even begin to tell him, anyway.

'How are you feeling?' he asked gently. 'Besides the obvious.'

Tears pricked her eyes again. After years of dealing with troubled young adults, her own father, and even the unkindness of Max's parents, she was used to the darker side of human nature. But sometimes other people demonstrated a depth of human kindness that was truly humbling. Not least the way her sister-in-law had stepped up to offer her a kidney, and then the way Annie and her brother had opened their home to her without question.

And now here was Max—the man with whom she'd shared little more than the most incredible and the only five-night stand of her life—and he had tracked her down here because he was a good person. How far would that goodness extend, though?

'Besides the obvious physical exhaustion?' she asked with a weak smile in a bid to buy herself more time. 'I'm feeling mentally drained.'

It might send him running, but at least then she would know.

Max said nothing. Instead, he stood up and crossed the room to sit next to her on the couch. She couldn't hold back the torrent of words any longer.

'There have just been tests. So many tests that I thought they would never end. Not to mention all the tests which Annie endured just to help me.' Evie lifted her hands to count off on her fingers. 'EKGs to check her heart rhythm, chest X-rays to rule out lung disease or lung tumours, pap smears and mammograms, CAT scans to check for kidney stones, not to mention a whole gamut of blood tests.'

She cast Max a sheepish glance.

'You'll already know that, I'm sorry. It's just I sometimes can't believe what she's put up with, for me.'

'You're important to her.' Max spoke quietly. 'And to your brother. Besides, you can't tell me you wouldn't have done the same thing for one of them.'

That was true. But it wasn't her doing it for them, was it?

'I just wish they didn't *have* to go through this for me. What if Annie gives me her kidney and her son needs it? She and my brother have a nine-year-old boy.'

'Is there any reason to think he would need it?' he asked calmly.

She knew what Max was getting at. PKD was usually inherited. Her nephew was about as healthy as wild, boisterous, vitality-filled nine-year-old boys got.

'My brother doesn't carry the gene, and my nephew was checked out and found clear. But that's not the point,' she objected. 'He could get hit by a car, develop some other undiagnosed kidney disorder, or anything.'

'Unlikely, given what you've just said,' Max soothed. 'Is that what happened with you? You only discovered you had a kidney disease this last year?'

Old memories crashed into Evie out of the blue, sideswiping her. Memories of her mother and her stepfather, and of her brother. How they'd rallied around her as a teenager when they'd first discovered there was a problem. She couldn't have hoped for a closer-knit family back then and, with Annie as her sister-in-law now, she was still so very fortunate. But she missed her parents. Almost every single day. Her heart ached for the fact that they would never even know about their granddaughter. Imogen would never have the incredible memories of loving grandparents that her nephew had.

'Evie?'

She'd been staring off into the distance. With a start, Evie dragged herself back to the present.

'Sorry. What were we saying?'

'Did you discover your illness this past year?'

'No,' she admitted, her eyes meeting his. 'I was diagnosed with polycystic kidney disease when I was a kid, but I only started entering the first stages of renal failure one year ago.'

That had been the same week she'd allowed herself to break her rules and sleep with Max.

'What happened?'

'I'd been working with a particularly troubled young boy when I got kicked.'

'That must have been some kick,' he growled.

'I guess.'

She wasn't about to tell him it had been so forceful it had propelled her several metres backwards across the office. The kick hadn't caused the problem, it had merely been a catalyst. She tried to lighten the tone.

'But it was right over the site of my weakest kidney. Murphy's law, I guess.'

'I see.' Max nodded grimly. 'No wonder you left your job. I would imagine that would have been a hard decision for you. I know how passionate you were about your work there.'

Evie frowned.

'I haven't left for good, I just took leave when I became too exhausted to work there.'

She wasn't prepared for his reaction.

'Evie, you can't possibly go back to work there.'

'Of course I can.' She bristled at his authoritative tone. 'As soon as I'm well again.'

If all was well again.

'Don't be stupid.' He snorted with derision. 'If this is what can happen to you before the transplant, think of the damage it could cause right over the site of a graft.'

Evie suppressed a shudder and folded her arms defiantly across her chest.

'Who do you think you are, ordering me around?'

'I'm not ordering you around.' He gritted his teeth at her, clearly trying to control his frustration.

They stared at each other in silence. Evie wondered whether, like her, Max was questioning how such an argument had come out of nowhere.

'I'm sorry.' Max held up his hands at last. 'You were telling me how you came to find out about your kidney disorder.'

'Right,' she acknowledged half-heartedly. 'We

knew from tests back then that my brother wasn't a match, but my mother had been, so…'

She tailed off, unable to finish the sentence. They'd always assumed her mother would be her donor when the time came. As if losing her mother hadn't been bad enough to start with.

'Your mother is no longer around?' Max surmised, the previous heat now gone from his voice.

'She died just before I moved to Silvertrees. Well, to the centre, you know?'

'I see,' he said again.

'It was a car crash,' she choked out, shaking her head.

Clearly he was taking everything she said on face value, listening to her as a friend, not as a surgeon.

He trusted her. She hadn't realised that before.

If he had his surgeon's hat on he wouldn't have assumed earlier that her high-level HLA sensitisation was a result of a previous transplant. He'd have registered that she was talking about end-stage renal failure now and not a previous transplant failing, which would leave him with only two other realistic possibilities for her high antibody levels in her PRA results. A blood transfusion, or the pregnancy.

But it wouldn't be long before he worked it out.

And Evie knew she had to get in there first and tell him about Imogen. His reactions this afternoon had shown more concern for her well-being than she could have imagined. Max wasn't as uninterested in her as she'd been led to believe.

'For what it's worth—' his voice cut through the silence '—I think the death of your mother, so close to your own recent diagnosis, is what's causing you not to think straight.'

'Think straight?'

'About Annie being your donor? I can tell you're having doubts, Evie. You're physically and emotionally worn out and you're getting cold feet because the operation is imminent. You know yourself how patients can get before an operation, any operation. I hope you're not considering refusing Annie's offer.'

She'd thought about it. A thousand times. But on the few occasions where she'd raised it with Annie, her sister-in-law had refused to listen, lovingly laying on the guilt as she reminded Evie that she was all Imogen had, and that she owed it to her daughter to accept the kidney.

'I'm not going to refuse. Annie wouldn't allow it,' Evie hiccupped. 'But it doesn't necessarily make it any easier.'

'It's called *the gift of life* for a reason, Evie.' He

stroked her hand gently. 'And I understand your initial concerns. But think of it this way—you're clearly a close family and you owe it to your niece and nephew to be the cool aunt you clearly already are to them.'

Evie froze, his words hurling spikes of ice down her spine.

'My niece?'

'I saw the photographs.'

He jerked his head to the bookshelf. Nausea churned up Evie's stomach. *This was it. She had to do it now.*

She couldn't find the words and the room swayed. She grabbed at the couch; the familiar feel of the piping on the cushion was comforting and she plucked at it absently.

'Evie? Are you okay?' His voice was sharp, his hand slipping into her hair to force her to look at him.

The hallway clock ticked audibly, outside the street was quiet—to anyone else it might even appear peaceful—a gaggle of geese passing noisily outside the window.

'Evie.' He snapped his fingers in front of her face.

Slowly she lifted her eyes to his.

'That's not my niece,' she whispered.

He looked surprised but still didn't understand. A gurgle of semi-hysterical laughter bubbled up inside her.

Max Van Berg, the high-flying surgeon who never missed a thing in a patient, was missing the one thing staring him right in the face.

'Imogen is my daughter.' Her eyes raked over his face, willing him to really hear what she was telling him. 'She's *your* daughter.'

CHAPTER THREE

'YOU HAVE A DAUGHTER?'

He knew the words were there but his brain didn't appear to be processing the message clearly. It might as well have been trying to work in a vat of thick treacle.

'*We* have a daughter,' Evie repeated tentatively.

Slowly, slowly, his brain began to pick up speed.

'I have a daughter,' he repeated, his hand dropping from Evie's hair as he pushed himself away from her. 'I have a three-month-old baby, and you didn't tell me until now?'

Evie crossed her arms over her chest, refusing to meet his eyes.

'Five months old,' she answered shakily.

'Sorry?'

'Imogen is five months old. Not three.'

He turned to pin her with a narrow gaze as she reached for his glass and took a generous gulp as though she was parched. It took a moment for him to register.

'That's enough,' he bit out, taking the juice from her and setting it out of reach before pushing himself up from the couch and moving over to the window, reinforcing the space between them.

'Drinking that won't help you,' he muttered, staring out at the uneventful street scene.

'Thank you,' she whispered so quietly he almost missed it.

He could certainly go for a drink himself. A drink of the large, stiff variety, not a glass of orange juice. And he rarely drank.

'We slept together a year ago. You're telling me the baby was two months premature?'

'That's not unusual given my…condition.'

He had to strain to hear her.

'The baby was born at thirty-two weeks? Thirty-three?'

'Thirty-two weeks. I went onto dialysis five days a week to carry her for as long as I could, but my body was under pressure, so they made the decision…'

Part of his brain told him that she'd done well to get that far. Her health would have been deteriorating rapidly as the growing foetus put more and more strain on her already stressed organs. It certainly explained why she'd gone from healthy when they were together a year ago, to being taken in for her transplant within the week.

'You never thought to…not to have it? For your health? For the baby's health?'

Even the words tasted bitter in his mouth.

He knew instantly that he'd said the wrong thing. If he'd felt he'd somehow passed some unknown test earlier, he knew he'd clearly fallen short of the mark now. A shuttered expression dropped over Evie's features and her voice turned cold.

'That's all I needed to know.' Her voice was shaking. Whether from anger or distress, he couldn't be sure, but his own emotions were too uprooted to care.

'Please leave, Max.'

How had this turned around so that she *was the one furious with* him?

He swung around incredulously.

'Really, Evangeline? For the last twelve months you have wilfully kept the knowledge of my baby from me, and now you're the one acting hard done by?'

'Because you've just told me you thought I should have…never had her.'

'Don't put words in my mouth,' he bit out. 'I was only concerned about the impact on your health as well as the baby's. You admitted yourself that the stress of carrying a baby was too much for your body and they had to carry out a C-section when it was only seven months old.'

'She.'

He looked at her in confusion.

'Pardon?'

'My baby is a *she*, not an *it*,' Evie choked out at him.

'Fine. *She*.' Had he really said *it*?

He hadn't meant to but he was still processing the news. Dead air compacted the room, making it hard to catch a deep breath. Hard even to think.

'So the baby is all right? She's well?'

The look of pride that lit up her eyes was unmistakeable.

'Yes, she's well.'

'How long was she in NICU?'

'Only thirty days. She weighed three pounds and four ounces when she was born. She needed to weigh around four and a half pounds, and be able to feed, breathe, and stay warm on her own before they would let her come home.'

'Of course,' he managed hollowly.

'She was actually pretty good at maintaining a good body temperature without the help of an incubator,' Evie babbled on. 'But she couldn't breathe and swallow at the same time, so feeding was the big issue.'

'Thirty days.' He blew out a deep breath at last. 'Our baby was in the NICU for thirty days and you never once called me. Never once tried to contact me. In fact, you didn't just need that single month to get in touch with me, Evie, you had seven months before that.'

Evie stared at him mutely.

'Nothing to say for yourself?'

'The snide tone is beneath you,' croaked Evie.

'Call it shock,' he bit back.

A bleak thought suddenly leapt out at him and he rounded on her.

'What do you want? Money?'

'No.'

He might have believed her cry of indignation five minutes earlier. Now, he didn't know what to believe.

'Really?'

'Do you…think I did this deliberately?' she croaked. 'To trap you?'

'Did you?' he demanded.

Her aghast look didn't sway him. He couldn't make sense of it.

'You told me categorically that you couldn't get pregnant.'

'I'd been told that was the case,' she replied weakly.

'Come on, Evie, we're both medical professionals. Just because you have PKD doesn't mean you can't have kids, it doesn't even mean you'd have necessarily developed renal failure. Plenty of women with PKD have one or two successful pregnancies without increasing their risk. In fact, the last figures I read suggested that only fifty per cent of people with PKD will have renal failure by the age of sixty, and about sixty per cent by the age of seventy. There's no reason to suggest you would have even had renal failure if you hadn't been kicked by that kid.'

Max stopped, hoping that was enough. Instead, Evie just stared at him as though she didn't recognise him, making him feel like the bad guy when, surely, it should be her?

'I didn't say I couldn't have children because of my PKD.'

Her voice cracked with emotion but she didn't elaborate. Max barely stifled his frustration.

'Then what? The dialysis?' He scrambled to calculate everything she'd told him. 'You said you went onto dialysis *after* you realised you were pregnant. But even if that hadn't been the case, the chances of a woman of child-bearing age falling pregnant whilst on dialysis are slim but not impossible, one to seven per cent, right? So however you spin it, there's no medical reason to support your assurances to me that it was impossible for you to get pregnant. So, I ask again, did you deliberately set out to trap me?'

Her desperate look disconcerted him more than he cared to admit.

'I would *never* have set out to trap you. Or anyone,' she defended herself. 'When I was diagnosed with PKD, I was also diagnosed with an ovulation disorder. I was told that I would likely need fertility treatment to conceive, which would only be given if my PKD wasn't a factor.'

'I see.' His brain felt as if it were working through treacle to process the information. How could he be sure she wasn't lying to him now? He took in her ashen pallor, her pinched nose, her shaking hands. Was he being churlish?

'I'm sorry. I should never have said all that.'

'No, you…you shouldn't have.'

'It doesn't make sense for you to have set out to trap me, to want money from me, because if you had then you'd have hit me up for it as soon as she was born. So at least you have that in your favour. But right now, it's the only thing you've got in your favour, Evie.'

'It's not that simple.'

'Yes, it *is* that simple. How could you have failed to tell me about the baby? If I hadn't had a plastics consult in that transplant unit yesterday, if I hadn't walked into that corridor at that moment, would you ever have sought me out to tell me about her?'

She didn't respond and the silence settled over them like a heavy shroud, bleak and suffocating. Trees moved in the breeze outside the window, creating a gap to allow the sunlight through. The heat warming up his back was a discordant sensation.

'Well, would you have?'

'I wanted to tell you.' She shook her head at last. 'But things were…are…more complicated than that.'

'Bull,' he snorted. 'I have a daughter. I deserve to have been told about her. *You* should have told me about her.'

'I wanted to…' Evie began uncertainly. 'But you were in Gaza and when I tried to—'

'That's pathetic, Evie,' Max cut her off. 'You could have found a way. You could've got a message to me if you'd wanted to.'

'It isn't that simple, Max. Please believe me.'

'Regardless of your claim that it isn't about money, I intend to meet my financial obligations.'

'I don't want you to do anything out of some

sense of obligation,' Evie cried. 'That's why I didn't tell you. Imogen and I don't need resentment in our lives because you never wanted to be drawn into a family.'

'And yet here I am.'

She pushed up off the couch with a sudden burst of energy and made for the living-room door. But it didn't escape him that she was clinging onto it for support as much as holding it open for him.

'Then let me make it clear that you're free to leave. I will never contact you again. Imogen will never need you.'

'It doesn't work that way.'

The harsh bark didn't sound like his own voice. His head was swimming, emotions he couldn't identify crowding his brain—all bar one.

Fear.

He was a highly regarded surgeon on his way to the top of his profession. He controlled crisis situations and managed people through some of the worst times in their life. He relished the feeling of being calm and in control.

None of that was helping him now. He hadn't felt such fear since he'd been a kid. Helpless and vulnerable. All because of his parents. He'd sworn he'd never have a family, never put a child of his through the hell that his parents had laid on him without them even meaning to. And Evie was offering him the chance to walk away from a situation he would never, ever have chosen to put himself into.

But the choice had been taken out of his hands. He was a father. There was a child out there who needed him to *be* that father. He could never turn his back and walk away.

But so help him he had no idea what he *was* supposed to do. The only thing he could do was begin with the practical, the bit he knew.

'I'll start making arrangements straight away.'

'What kind of arrangements?'

'I told you.' He straightened his shoulders. 'Financial arrangements.'

'And I told you that we don't need your money.'

'Look around you, Evie. You're living in your brother's home, which is barely big enough for *his* family, and you've got a baby of your own. *My* baby. You need money. My daughter needs money.'

'The only thing my baby needs right now is love. And I have plenty of that. Clearly, you don't.'

And just like that, Evie hit on his darkest fear.

She was right, he thought, about providing for his daughter materially, but beyond that he *didn't* know how to love anyone. How could he?

He'd been given everything that a child could materially need, but he'd never learned what it was like to *be* loved.

Evie watched her knuckles turn white as she clung on to the door for all she was worth. He'd talked about *obligations* and *arrangements*. All the same things his parents had so calmly and logically presented to her. It seemed they were right after all: they knew their son better than Evie did. Of course they did. And they had been right that he didn't want a child in his life.

And she knew how damaging it would be for him to stay only to resent her and Imogen every day that he was in their lives. Better for him to go now. But Max didn't look as though he had any intention of leaving. Instead he started pacing the floor as he raked his hands through his hair.

'If you and Annie are due at Silvertrees for the transplant within the next few days, what's happening with Imogen?' Max demanded abruptly.

What did that have to do with it?

'My brother will look after Imogen.' She couldn't keep the shake out of her voice. 'Although I'll be at Silvertrees, Annie will undergo her operation at her local hospital. She should be able to be discharged within a matter of days, so it'll be easier for her to be nearer home.'

'Whereas you'll be kept in for longer, and the transplant team at Silvertrees will want to do as many of your follow-ups as possible themselves, before transferring you back to a local unit.'

'Right.'

'So I'm guessing they'll complete the nephrectomy on Annie in the morning, prepare the kidney for transport to Silvertrees and operate on you by the afternoon?' he guessed.

What was his point?

'Yes, I think that's the plan,' she replied stiffly. 'Obviously the Silvertrees team need to monitor me closely but with any luck it will go smoothly, the kidney will start working straight away, I won't need dialysis and I'll be out and back home with Imogen within a week.'

'And your check-ups?' He frowned, unconvinced. 'Even if you are discharged that quickly, and frankly I think you're being unrealistic, you'll need to go in every couple of days for the first week or so, then at least twice a week for several weeks after that. To ensure your body isn't rejecting the new kidney and to balance your immunosuppressants.'

'I'll make the journey.' She jutted her chin out

mutinously. She wasn't going to stay in hospital, away from her daughter, any longer than she had to.

'You won't be able to drive, so you're going to ask your brother to drive a three-hour round trip every couple of days? Taking a five-month-old baby with you? Unless you're planning on leaving her with Annie, of course, who'll still be recovering herself? Or are you intending that all four of you make the journey?'

He was angry, and he had every right to be, but every cruelly thrown word felt like a physical blow. She knew it was asking a lot of Annie, of her brother, but what choice was there? This conversation was painful, and she didn't see it getting them anywhere other than the mess they had now.

'You've already made your position pretty clear, Max. And that's fine. You didn't ask for this, and I gave you no say in the matter. But I'm releasing you now, from any obligations relating to our baby. You have my word I will never come to you again.'

'I'm not walking away from the baby,' Max snarled at her.

The fire in his eyes could have burned the house down around her.

'I am this baby's father, and I will not allow you to push me out of her life now. I won't allow you to let her grow up thinking her father didn't want her. I *will* be there, whenever she needs me.'

It could have just been grand rhetoric but there was an unshakeable resolve behind the words, which made Evie take stock. And Max looked just as stunned as she felt.

Maybe she needed to remember what a shock this must all be to him, learning about his daughter, and her own kidney transplant, all at once. It had been a big enough shock to her and she'd had the advantage that it had all been staggered over the last year, at least.

And hadn't shock also made her act in a way she'd almost instantly regretted, when she'd taken the money from his parents the day after Imogen's birth?

Yet as a low cry began from the room down the hallway Evie was spared the need to respond to his declaration.

'Imogen,' she cried, scrambling out of the room.

She moved quickly down the narrow hallway to the temporary bedroom she shared with her daughter, but as she became aware of Max following her an image of his luxury designer home came to mind. Spacious and minimalist, it screamed wealth. All the things she didn't have—not if she was going to stick to her promise to herself that the cheque his parents had thrown at her would be kept in a trust for Imogen in the event that Evie's transplant didn't work. But money that Max, as he'd so pointedly reminded her earlier, *could* offer Imogen. In spades.

'Wait back there,' she sputtered.

'You've got no chance.'

With the cry of objection at being left alone becoming more insistent, she didn't have time to argue further. Stuffing down the sense that she couldn't offer their daughter the kind of home to grow up in that Max must have enjoyed, Evie set her teeth and continued down the short hallway and into her room.

She practically had to climb over her single bed to get to Imogen's hand-me-down cot, sniffing the air, which smelled, as always, of lavender baby bubble bath and aloe vera baby lotion. Although, to Max's sensitised nose, she couldn't help fearing it would somehow smell of baby sick or dirty nappies, giving her yet another area in which she fell short in his eyes.

But as soon as the tiny, flushed, screwed-up face saw her and eased into a wide smile Evie forgot their surroundings. She lifted up Imogen, cradling the baby to her chest, and inhaled her unique baby smell.

She would never let anyone take her daughter from her, no matter how much money they had.

By the time she turned around, Max was standing braced against the doorjamb and apparently unsure whether to come in or stay put as he searched for somewhere, anywhere, to place his feet. This time, she wouldn't be intimidated.

'This is where you both sleep?'

She feigned a casual shrug.

'It used to be their downstairs office. They made it a bedroom for Imogen and I because upstairs is only two-bed and I wasn't about to turf either them or my nine-year-old nephew out of their bedrooms.'

'No need to sound so defensive.'

'No need to look so appalled,' she quipped, holding Imogen tighter.

He stepped back, allowing her to shuffle her way through the gap and back to the doorway, but she noticed he didn't offer to take the baby. His daughter. *Was she relieved or hurt?*

'So this is where you expect to return to after your transplant?'

'So?'

'So, given that you aren't supposed to bend and lift anything for around six weeks after your operation, you think you're going to be able to vault that makeshift cot-bed, and stretch down to pick up your five-month-old daughter?'

'I'll have help.' She didn't intend to sound so mutinous, but dammit if she hadn't handed him his argument on a silver platter.

'Help being your sister-in-law, who's having an operation to give you a kidney and who also shouldn't be bending and lifting?' Max clarified. 'Or help from your brother, who I presume will also be trying to look after his wife and son? And what about his work?'

'We'll figure it out,' Evie snapped back, not wanting him to see how close to the mark he was.

What choice did they have? At least, mercifully, he fell silent as he followed her back up the corridor. However, as she turned to the living room Max continued to the front door. She couldn't conceal her shock.

'You're leaving?'

'Yes.'

'Just like that?' she gasped.

'I have things to do.'

Dumbfounded, all Evie could do was stare. She'd told him he was free to leave; she meant it. But for him to do so when Imogen, his daughter, was right there, for him not to even want to see her or hold her...

It was as if her heart were being torn out. She buried her head against her daughter and rained tiny kisses all over her precious skin. Right then she swore never to let Imogen feel unloved or unwanted.

So much for Max's promise to do the same.

'I'll be back by six o'clock tomorrow night.'

She froze.

'I… What do you mean…?'

'What I said.' He huffed out a breath. 'Make sure you and Imogen are packed. I'll pick you up six o'clock tomorrow.'

'Why?'

'Because you're both coming to live with me.'

For the second time in as many minutes Evie couldn't make her vocal cords work. All she could do was shake her head in objection.

'Don't test me, Evangeline,' Max warned. 'This is best for you and for Imogen. You and your sister-in-law both need to heal after your operations and you need to be close to Silvertrees for the next three months or until your nephrology team clear you after the transplant. And at least at mine, you won't risk hurting yourself clambering over your bed to get to Imogen's cot.'

'Live with you for three months? Why would you do that?'

And why was a weak part of her so tempted, in spite of everything?

'Because I'm the baby's father, Evangeline.' He stuffed down his exasperation. 'It's *my* responsibility, too. Not some stranger's.'

'Annie's family. Not some stranger. And you're a surgeon who's only interested in focusing on his career. You told me that yourself. You don't have time to look after a baby.'

'Then I'll damn well make time. Just like I did to come down here. I'll take holidays—I'm certainly owed them.'

Evie blinked in shock. This felt so unexpected. Max was always so careful, so measured. She'd thought she'd known him well enough to believe he would be responsible enough to be a distant father to Imogen, but not that he would take full responsibility for them both.

'So, pack whatever clothes and belongings you and Imogen need, a few suitcases at most. I'll be back tomorrow night to pick you up.'

'Max—'

'Six o'clock tomorrow evening, Evie. No arguments, no stalling, just be ready. Both of you.'

CHAPTER FOUR

'WHAT HAPPENED TO your car?' Evie blurted out as she followed Max down the front steps. Imogen was in her arms, their cases in his.

He suppressed a grim response, confining himself to the barest minimum of responses as he loaded the bags into the new car.

'I traded it in last night.'

She didn't even try to disguise her gasp of shock.

'Who willingly swaps out his pride and joy sports car?'

He resisted the urge to tell her that it was a supercar, not merely a sports car. Buying his first one ten years ago had signified the moment he'd decided he'd arrived as a surgeon, and every time he'd driven it to and from the hospital it had been the payoff for everything else he would sacrifice for his career. Yet the truth was he'd never felt so ambivalent towards his car from the moment yesterday when he'd walked out of that suburban house—a father.

The satisfaction he'd got from driving the sleek car on his outbound journey hadn't been with him on his homeward trek. In fact, from the moment he'd walked back out into the street and taken another look at all the family cars on the various driveways, he'd realised his whole life had been turned upside down and inside out.

He was a father. The life he'd grown up envisaging for himself was gone for ever.

And somehow, the thought hadn't chagrined him the way he might have expected.

'It was a matter of practicality.' He offered a deliberately nonchalant shrug. 'It wasn't a car designed for a baby seat. Whereas this is a decent family car.'

'Decent? It's one of the most luxurious, top-of-the-range family cars I've ever seen. And you swapped it out overnight? Just like that?' Evie sniffed but he refused to take the bait.

'Just like that, yes. But don't worry,' he added sarcastically, 'I've still made sure all optional extras are included. Any other questions?'

'Plenty.' She clicked her tongue nervously but he could see she was still disconcerted.

He waited until she had finished settling the baby into the baby seat in the back, waiting until she stood back up, closed the rear door carefully and moved to the front passenger door.

'What's the problem, Evie?' He reined in his frustration.

She paused, frowning as she cast another eye over the vehicle.

'I don't want you resenting me. Us. And you will, if you go sacrificing things like your car. Besides, it's only for a few days.'

The irony wasn't lost on Max. He barked out a humourless laugh.

'You kept the existence of my daughter from me, Evangeline. If I hadn't seen you in that hospital corridor two days ago I still wouldn't know about my daughter. And yet you think it would be the fact that I had to give up my *car* which would make me resent you?'

'You resent me?' She turned to him bleakly.

'You weren't going to tell me about the baby, Evie. What the hell do you expect?'

The raw expression on her face turned to one of annoyance.

'It's Imogen.'

'Pardon?'

'We had this conversation yesterday when you insisted on calling her *it*,' Evie sniped. 'Now I'm reminding you that your daughter's name is Imogen. Not *the baby.*'

Had he really just heard her correctly?

'Are you serious?'

'If you're going to take the moral high ground with me, then, yes, I'm serious. You act like your daughter actually means something to you, yet you can't even call her by her name.'

He bit his tongue before he could say any more, sliding into the driver's seat as he fought against a fresh burst of the darkest rage he'd ever known in his life. It had been bubbling constantly, barely below the surface, since yesterday. But he had to control it. If he came on too heavy and scared Evie off, he might lose his daughter. He might never have intended to have a family, but he was more determined than ever that, now he had a daughter, she would never grow up feeling, well, not unwanted exactly, but certainly inadequate. Unloved.

He allowed his mind to wander for a moment. Back to his past, and back to his own parents. *Didn't they used to call him* the baby *or* the boy? Never Max. And certainly never an endearment. He'd hated it, so why was he now calling his own daughter *the baby*? It was galling, but Evie was right.

His parents had given him a good home, nice

room, toys, even time as long as it was for academic work. But they'd never had time to come to a rugby match, a swim meet, a school play. Work had always come first. And he'd always known that it was the most important thing in their lives. They'd told him. Sat him down and explained it to him, told him that he was mature enough to understand them and that when he too was a successful surgeon he'd feel exactly the same way. As if a seven-year-old boy could understand that.

'Look, arguing isn't going to get us anywhere.'

Max had never found it so difficult to keep his voice even and calm. He held his hands up in placation as Evie climbed cautiously into the passenger seat.

'We have to find a way past the anger. For her sake if no one else.'

He dipped his head slightly to indicate the baby gurgling obliviously in the back of the car.

'I agree,' Evie acknowledged, her voice still quivering slightly. 'I'm sorry I sniped at you.'

'Right.'

'And I'm sorry I didn't tell you about Imogen. You have no idea how sorry. If I could go back and change things, I truly would. I wish I'd been able to tell you a long time ago.'

'Then why didn't you?' he asked as non-combatively as he could.

'I tried…' She tailed off, her eyes fixed straight ahead, unable to meet his. 'It's…complicated. And I know that sounds feeble but, believe me, I'm trying to find the words to explain myself.'

'Thank you,' he said simply.

Her spontaneous apology was the acknowledgement he'd been waiting for. To know that she knew what she'd done had been wrong. That he'd had a right to know about his baby from the start.

Yet deep down, as the heat of rage was finally ceasing to sear, he was beginning to try to understand her motivations.

'Was it because of your kidney transplant?'

'Sorry?' He saw her head turn to him in his peripheral vision as the engine roared into life.

'Was your kidney transplant the reason you didn't tell me when you first discovered you were pregnant? Did you think I'd insist you put your health first? That you should have a termination?'

A beat of silence.

'Wouldn't you have?' she challenged unsteadily.

Another beat of silence whilst he thought.

'I would have recommended it. Carrying a baby to term for a healthy woman is stressful enough on her body, but, given your kidney disease, it makes sense medically,' he acknowledged. 'But I would never have insisted. Ultimately, that had to be your decision. And I would have preferred to have supported you through the pregnancy.'

He heard her intake of breath.

'You were in Gaza and out of reach.'

'You could have got hold of me if you'd wanted. You knew who I was working with. You'd have had only to contact their head office and they could have got a message to me.'

'I can't imagine you'd have appreciated that call in the middle of your mission out there.'

Max frowned. *Where did she get this unfavourable image of him from?*

'You don't know me at all, do you? I'd rather have known. Just like you, I'd rather have had the option to make decisions for myself. To cut the tour short and come home if I saw fit to do so.'

'I never thought of that.' The words were so quiet, said more to herself to him, that Max almost missed them.

He still had no idea how the baby…Imogen… was going to fit into his life, but he knew that he needed to buy himself some time whilst he figured it out. Evie certainly thought it was a temporary arrangement, and, whilst he agreed with her on that score, he knew it was going to be a couple of months—rather than a couple of weeks—before she would be recovered enough to think about living on her own again. But by then he should have had time to work out a long-term solution, because she was seriously mistaken if she thought he didn't want some kind of relationship with his daughter from here on out. He just had no idea how they were going to achieve it.

'There are very few things you need to know about me, Evie,' he told her firmly. 'I like things straightforward and honest, but I can't abide people making choices which impact heavily on me, without involving me in the decision-making process. Without even consulting me first.'

He'd had enough of that through his childhood to last him a lifetime. Not that Evie needed to know any of that. The contradiction wasn't lost on him.

'Consulting you...?' she echoed slowly.

'I won't accept it, Evangeline,' he stated grimly, struggling to shut out the ruthless memories. 'Do you understand?'

'But, Max—'

'There are no *ifs* or *buts*, Evie,' he spat out, more at himself.

At his own weakness that even after all this time it should still affect him the way that it did. How had this situation with Evie raked up so much hurt that he'd convinced himself he'd long since buried? Shifting in his seat, Max strived to recover his famed dispassion and composure, but it seemed to have deserted him as he opened his mouth again.

'That's the one thing I absolutely won't tolerate.'

She hadn't thought her heart could beat any faster or harder in her chest, every word like a nail in the coffin of her integrity.

How could she possibly tell him about the cheque and his parents now? Decisions that had been made with the express purpose of keeping Max in the dark? Believing she was doing the best thing she could for her daughter.

Evie pressed her shoulders into the plush leather seat back and drew deep breaths. *In through the nose, out through the mouth. In through the nose, out through the mouth.* One minute went by. Then five. Then ten. The nausea subsided a fraction, nothing more.

If she didn't tell him it would only make it harder to do so later. But—after what he'd just said—what if he turned around and sent her and Imogen back home straight away? She might not have shown Max her gratitude at taking her in, but she was indebted to him for the opportunity to allow Annie and her family some space to recover, as well as allowing herself to stay within easy reach of Silvertrees for the first few weeks after the transplant.

Worse still. What if she told him the truth and he tried to take Imogen away from her? She didn't think that was the kind of man Max was, but how could she be sure? Between her actions in taking the bribe, and her precarious health, could a judge decide that her daughter was better off with Max than with herself? Out of the two of them, *she* was the one who would appear to have acted unscrupulously. How had *that* happened?

She didn't realise they'd lapsed into silence for the last half an hour until his voice, deep and smooth and as self-assured as ever, broke into her thoughts.

'I saw one of your troubled teens the other day.'

'At Silvertrees?' She craned her neck to look at him, grateful for his efforts to find a more neutral topic for them to discuss.

'A young lad, in for a consult,' confirmed Max.

'Do you know who it was?'

'Vince Morrison. The sixteen-year-old with gynaecomastia.'

'They're finally allowing him to get surgery? That's great—psychologically he really needs it.'

'No, the parents came in to get more information

but they left, deciding it was better to wait until he was older again.'

Evie gave a grunt of frustration.

'That wasn't the outcome you'd been hoping for?' Max asked.

'No.' She rubbed one hand over her eyes. 'Vince's deteriorating behaviour in school and at home brought him to us at the centre a couple of years ago. He's lucky, he has a loving family and kind parents, and they were trying to do their best for him. But, honestly, they were despairing as the gentle child they had known had begun to be replaced by a boy they could barely recognise.'

'I imagine he didn't understand what was happening to his body? Probably getting bullied in school.'

'Yep. The boys had been taunting him with the name Moob Boy, taking photos on their mobiles in the changing rooms and texting them around the school. He started fighting and skipping classes. He'd been a keen swimmer—Schools International—and all that stopped. He wouldn't go on beach holidays with his family, or to rugby camp. He was struggling mentally and physically.'

It felt like it had felt in the early days, before they'd slept together. The easy way they'd always been able to discuss cases.

'The procedure to remove the abnormal breast tissue is fairly straightforward—why would there be a problem?'

'I don't know.' Evie threw her hands up. 'His parents thought it was a phase, that he might grow into his body, and that he should learn to live with it until he was eighteen. I felt the psychological damage might be too great by then, and that it was an unnecessary wait.'

'I would have agreed with you,' Max stated.

The simple admission warmed her insides. She could really use that compliment from him right now.

'So do you know why they went for the consult if they weren't going to go ahead with it?' she asked, feeling less troubled for the first time since they'd left the house.

'By all accounts, their son took the family car in the middle of the night and ended up crashing into a wall. They came to listen to what the paediatric surgeon had to say but didn't like the idea of putting him through the surgery. I couldn't understand why, but now you've explained their attitude beforehand, it makes sense.'

'Who was the paediatric surgeon? Couldn't they have talked the parents round? Explained things?'

'Not enough knowledge of the boy's mental-health history.'

'Why not?' Evie frowned. 'Where were all my notes?'

'It's not your notes they needed. It's the passion, the conviction. *You're* what sells these cases, not a set of emotionless black and white notes.'

'Well, what about my replacement?'

'No one can replace you,' Max said, then coughed as he realised the way it sounded.

She felt the flush tingling from her toes to her legs, into her torso and up. It might not have been what he meant, but it felt good to hear nonetheless.

'Listen, how about I go to the centre and speak to the manager, see if I can't get him to set up a meeting with the Morrisons?' Max offered, his professional tone firmly in place. 'Give them my professional opinion and go from there?'

'That would mean a lot, especially to Vince. But why would you do that for me, Max?'

She knew he'd started the conversation in order to find some common ground between them. Talking about the case was the first real conversation they'd had without awkwardness or disagreement in the last forty-eight hours and it felt like a real step forward. Proof that they *could* work together and agree on a solution that would be in their daughter's best interests.

'I want to do it to show how I appreciate your earlier apology,' Max said unexpectedly. 'And I think it's time I made one of my own.'

'An apology?'

'I feel I guilted you into coming to stay with me. As though you owed it to me for not telling me about the baby. Deep down, I think I can understand some of your reasons even if I don't agree. But I wanted you to know this isn't just about the baby...sorry, Imogen...this is about wanting to help you, too.'

'Really?'

She watched him carefully, surprised as he took his eyes off the road for a moment to meet hers.

'Yes, Evie, really.' He turned back to the road. 'I think you should stay with me because I think it will be better for your recovery to stay close to Silvertrees for as long as possible, in order to be checked over by the transplant team themselves, rather than being handed off to a follow-on team too early.'

'And you do *want* to get to know your daughter, right?' She had to check.

'Of course I do. It's important to me that my daughter knows she is loved and never feels she wasn't wanted. More important than I think you can realise. To that end, I want to make sure I do what's best for her, yes.'

He was choosing his words carefully, but it wasn't necessarily helping her. Was he alluding to his parents? She couldn't even ask, without revealing her own experience of them. It left Evie feeling thwarted.

'Which brings me back around to how you and I are going to proceed from here.'

'You and I?' Her mouth felt suddenly dry again.

'You and I,' he confirmed calmly. 'I'll admit I've been angry that I didn't know about Imogen before now, and I've been punishing you for it. I was too wrapped up in myself to consider that you've got enough to deal with at the moment with your imminent transplant without additional stress from me.'

Evie squirmed in her seat. This was the perfect opportunity to admit the truth to him.

'You do have every right to be mad...' she began.

'Maybe so, but it won't help you get through this transplant. You know as well as I do that a patient's mental well-being can influence not only how their body copes during the operation itself, but how their recovery goes afterwards. In your case, how your body responds—or rather doesn't—to a foreign organ.'

'I'll be fine,' she managed shakily, not fooling him for a moment.

'I understand that you've felt like you have to stay strong for your family all this time, especially with Annie being your donor. But you can let go a little now and lean on me.'

Hope flickered tentatively, but she still couldn't relax.

'You must still be angry, Max.'

'Evie, I don't know what happened, or why you... didn't get in touch. But I'm not going to push you on it any more. However, when you're ready to talk to me, I'd like that.'

'As easily as that?' She tried not to feel suspicious.

'Why not? We can't dwell on what's happened if we want to find the best future for our daughter.'

It sounded too good to be true, but Evie wasn't about to spoil it by arguing. It didn't change the real issues, not least the money, or the fact that she still hadn't told him about it. But it did go some way to re-establishing a rapport between the two of them so that, when she *did* eventually find the right moment and place to confess, Max wouldn't be so inflexible and impersonal in how he reacted to everything she needed to tell him.

She just needed to buy herself, and Imogen, some time.

'You can't go forwards into the past,' she said softly.

'Say again?'

She startled, not realising she'd said it aloud.

'Oh, nothing. It was just something my mum used to say. You can't go forwards into the past.'

She listened as Max repeated it, mulling the words over as he did so.

'It's a good way to put it.' He smiled. 'So, what do you think, Evie?'

'I think,' she began thoughtfully, 'I'd appreciate that very much.'

'So, friends?'

Evie licked her lips and offered him the first genuine smile since their five nights together.

'Friends.'

CHAPTER FIVE

'THAT'S ANOTHER FAIL,' Max exclaimed to his baby daughter as he lifted her off the changing mat only to watch the downward drop of his third nappy attempt in as many minutes.

This was his first morning in charge of his daughter, having taken Imogen off Evie late last night and telling Evie to get a full night's sleep. The drugs Evie would be on for the transplant made breastfeeding an impossibility, so he'd felt free to take Imogen and give her a feed in the night, subsequently going through more nappies than he cared to count trying to change her. Unsurprisingly, his daughter didn't look overly impressed with his performance so far.

He was a skilled, sought-after surgeon—how the heck could a tiny scrap of absorbent material for a tiny baby defeat him? He wasn't accustomed to failing at things, and he didn't like the feeling one bit.

'Right, nothing else for it.'

He carried Imogen over to the LCD home automation panel on the wall. 'Hmm...' he murmured, flicking through the online tutorials. 'Here we go: *Changing a baby's nappy.*'

To her credit, Imogen didn't cry but simply watched him with big, clear, expressive eyes, which were perfect replicas of her mother's, but it didn't make Max feel any more relaxed around her.

Funny, but he'd dealt with babies week in, week out in a medical and surgical setting, not least with all the work he'd done with the charity, from cleft lips and palates to club-feet, burns to reconstructive. But he'd never changed a nappy. He'd never wanted to change a nappy. That much hadn't changed. He was beginning to realise that his solution of looking after the baby, *his daughter*, whilst Evie was in hospital might not have been one of his most inspired ideas. He clearly wasn't cut out for it and being in charge of such a tiny life, outside the comfort of the operating theatre, was a weighty responsibility.

'Having trouble?'

He swung around, cradling Imogen against his chest as he did so.

'We're fine.'

'So I see.' She grinned, gesturing first to the

tutorial, then to the nappy, which was partly over Imogen's hip and partly over her knee.

'Okay,' he conceded sheepishly. 'So I might have a few things to learn. Anyway, you're meant to be resting.'

He'd insisted on giving her his master suite so that she could get as much rest as possible before her transplant, whilst he moved into the second bedroom, with the annexed dressing room now a nursery.

'I am resting. I forgot how comfortable your bed was—' She stopped abruptly, flushing a deep red.

Max quickly shut down any memories of the last time—the only other time—Evie had been in his home. Those five, intense days.

'Wait, *this* is Imogen's nursery?'

'It is.' He stepped back to let her have a full look around. 'Do you like it?'

'It's very…expensive-looking.'

It should be. He'd paid handsomely to have a designer come in and transform the room in one day, with less than twelve hours' notice. Still, he surveyed the room again, this time through Evie's eyes. It occurred to him that it was very different from the makeshift yet altogether cosier homely set-up she and Imogen had shared at her brother's house.

The interior designer had insisted on an oak sleigh cot, matching oak changing table—fully stocked—and oak wardrobe. A jungle theme ran throughout—Max having just about talked her out of a princess theme—from the bedding to the curtains, and the pastel walls with bright jungle mural to add some interest. On one wall a bookshelf overflowed with soft toys and books.

'I don't know why there are so many books.' He shrugged. 'It isn't as though Imogen will be reading for a while.'

'No, but it'll be nice to sit on that wicker chair over there and read to her at night.' Evie offered him a warm smile, but there was a hint of sadness behind it.

'I hadn't really thought of that,' he admitted with surprise.

'My mum used to have this big chair she called the reading chair, and at night we'd snuggle together and she would read to us for hours and hours. Even as a baby I think she used it to get us into the habit of reading.'

That would be why the idea hadn't occurred to him. He couldn't remember either of his parents reading to him. Ever. They'd always been too busy.

'How about *your* mum?'

'What?' he asked sharply, before checking himself.

'Did your mum read to you, too? Is that why you thought to put the chair and the books in here?'

He peered at her closely but there was nothing in her expression but innocence and interest. Slowly the tense feeling receded.

She hadn't meant anything by it—how could she have? She didn't know the first thing about his parents, and he intended to keep it that way.

'I don't recall,' he lied. 'She probably did. But it was the interior decorator who did this room.'

He didn't want his parents to have anything to do with his daughter. He didn't want them to create the same lack of self-worth in their grandchild as they had in him throughout his childhood. He'd been lucky to have that one teacher who had seen what was going on and taken a young Max under his wing. He wouldn't be a surgeon—a top surgeon, no less—without that one gentle, guiding hand.

'Oh, right, of course.' Evie accepted his explanation without question, and he felt simultaneously relieved and guilty.

'So, what are they like?' she asked.

'Who?'

'Your parents. Are they in the medical profession like you? Is that where you got such skills from? And the way you care so much for your patients?'

'No, it wasn't.' He just about held back the bitterness from his tone.

Of all people, his parents could have been his teachers, his heroes. They had expected him to follow them into a surgical career, and they'd certainly pushed him on the academic side. But they had never shown him a caring or loving side. He sometimes wondered why they had even bothered to have a kid, but the answer was simple: it had been expected. It hadn't been something they'd wanted.

Not that he was about to load his, or his parents', shortcomings onto Evie. She didn't need to know any of this.

In fact, he was beginning to realise that they didn't really know anything about each other at all. Evie was the mother of his baby and yet they might as well have been strangers. Maybe, if they were really serious about being friends for the sake of their daughter then he should actually start talking to her, asking about her life and her family. He had to admit, he was interested.

Max observed in silence as she watched her daughter, her eyes filled with affection. Her innate love for Imogen was beyond doubt. It made him feel…good, just to see it. Almost subconsciously, she skimmed her lower abdomen with her hand and he knew immediately what was going through her mind. He'd seen it time and again with his patients over the years.

'You're going to be fine,' he said quietly. Convincingly.

She shot him an unconvincing smile in return.

'I hope so. Thanks to Annie. Just as long as my body doesn't reject the new kidney.'

'You can't afford to think that way, Evie. You have to stay mentally strong. Be positive.'

'I know.' She bobbed her head but the way her shoulders hunched told a different story. 'But let's be fair, Max, we're effectively trying to disguise a foreign organ from my body. My PRA levels were high enough to warrant plasmapheresis. If my body spots it, it'll really attack it.'

'You know it's more complicated than that,' Max began, then stopped. Even doctors were allowed to get scared; it wouldn't help to simply censor everything Evie said.

He searched for something more constructive to say. To help her. But everything that came to mind didn't encapsulate what he wanted to tell her. He'd dropped pat phrases to patients and their families throughout his career, given them words of comfort whilst being sure not to make promises he couldn't fulfil. Promising to do everything he could for a patient wasn't the same as promising them that everything would be okay, because he *would* do everything he could but the outcome would never be exactly the same because every patient was different.

He had no way of knowing how Evie's body would react to the transplant. He couldn't say what the future held. Yet right now, for the first time in his life, he had to hold himself back from pulling Evie into his arms and promising her that everything was going to be okay.

He'd never wanted to believe it so much in his life.

Max cradled Imogen closer, grateful for occupying his hands and the inadvertent barrier she created between himself and Evie.

'All I can promise you is that you're in good hands. Arabella Goodwin is one of the best nephrologists in her field,' he declared brightly. 'All the tests and pre-op care she has carried out, the method she has selected for the transplant itself, the balance of immuno-suppressants, they're all to maximise your chance of success.'

'I know that.' Evie nodded and bit her lip. 'Logically, as a doctor, I know it. But as a patient, I hate not being the one in control.'

He could relate to that.

'So, forget you're a doctor for ten minutes and pretend you're a patient like any other. Talk it through like any other patient would.'

'How do you mean?'

'You're scared.'

She was going to argue, he could see it. Then she changed her mind.

'I *am* scared, yes. My body's antibodies are so high. The plasmapheresis is just to get me even close to being able to undergo the transplant, but after the operation there's bound to be more.'

'So think of it like both the transplant and the induction drugs are a mortgage deposit, and the maintenance drugs are your monthly mortgage payments. The bigger your initial deposit, the lower your monthly repayments need to be. In other words, the better the transplant takes and your body responds to those initial immuno-suppressants, the less chance your body will reject the kidney in the future, so the less maintenance drugs you're going to need.'

'It doesn't mean that a month, six months, twelve months down the road, my body might not suddenly decide to reject it.' She sucked in a breath.

'No, but we have to start somewhere. There's no way to predict who will suffer a rejection episode, but if you do we adjust the medication to attempt to reverse it. You know that a good percentage of transplant patients go through at least one rejection episode but it's mild enough to counter.'

'I know, and some patients have the same transplanted kidney twenty, forty years down the road, and might have had a handful of rejection episodes they've been able to reverse.'

'Right, and the lower your maintenance drugs are, the more room we have to play with to increase them.'

'Yes.'

Without warning, Evie smiled.

'You know, I actually *do* feel a bit better about it all.'

'Good.'

One little word, which didn't come close to how he was feeling. She looked genuinely less tense and his chest swelled a little to think that, together, they'd talked it out.

It wouldn't be the last time she'd need to run through things, to steady herself, but he'd be here for her every time she needed him. But right now, she needed him to move on.

'Are you hungry? If you fancy it I could make something to eat?'

She hesitated.

'It isn't a problem to make breakfast,' he cajoled.

'Breakfast would be nice.' Evie finally held her hands out. 'Shall I sort out Imogen's nappy?'

Max looked at the falling nappy and grinned wryly.

'I'll learn soon enough.'

The buzz of contact as he handed their daughter to Evie caught him off guard. Quickly he retreated to his temporary bedroom to snatch up a fresh tee shirt from the drawer before heading to the safety of downstairs.

Evie watched him go, her heart beating faster.

He'd lied to her. And she didn't know what it meant.

She'd been right that he had a complicated relationship with his parents. But she didn't know whether to be relieved that he clearly didn't have much time for his parents, or concerned that he clearly didn't intend to talk to her about it. The way the topic had come up so naturally had seemed like a good opportunity to ease her way into admitting the truth.

But if Max wasn't prepared to tell her even the

first thing about them, then how could she possibly admit she'd met them, let alone that they had paid her to keep his daughter from Max?

And yet, as awful as it sounded, wasn't it better that he didn't appear to be close to them given their utter indifference to their granddaughter? Having experienced both sides of it herself, a loving home with her mother and stepfather, and a difficult relationship trying not to antagonise her father, she knew she would have been just as well off if her father had never been around at all.

She dropped her head to her daughter's. She'd do anything to protect her baby from anyone who could hurt her, mentally or physically.

Almost in response, Imogen reached up and grabbed Evie's cheeks in her chubby little hands, smacking loud kisses onto her mother's face before burying her head into Evie's neck and nuzzling.

Evie's heart swelled. It was a feeling like no other. It hadn't bypassed her that although Max was clearly comfortable holding a baby from his time as a surgeon, skilled enough to be able to keep them calm and confident enough to examine them, he was detached about it. His daughter might as well have been any baby in his care. There was no bond.

Was it just a question of time? Or would there never be a special father-daughter bond there?

What would happen when she was in hospital? In this particular unit? Between going in for the pre-op and the transplant itself, she would be kept in a sterile environment where Imogen wouldn't be allowed to visit for at least a week. Maybe longer.

Her daughter had spent her life being showered with love, kisses, constant affection. From herself, her brother, Annie, even her nephew. Evie had no doubt that Max would meet Imogen's physical needs. But what about those emotional needs? She would need to see him soften towards Imogen, to look at her as his daughter rather than just a baby on whom he was going to operate, before she would be comfortable about being separated from her daughter for so long.

She was just going to have to teach Max how to show his emotions. The prospect filled her with both trepidation and exhilaration. *How exactly was that going to complicate things between the two of them?*

And teaching him how to change a nappy properly wouldn't be a bad idea, either. She stifled a giggle.

'Come on, precious girl. Let's get you sorted

out, and find you a pretty baby suit, then we'll go downstairs and show your daddy how neat and tidy you look.'

Evie sniffed appreciatively as she entered the kitchen where Max was cooking on the stove.

'Barely five minutes and something already smells heavenly.' She grinned.

'Imogen's crying,' Max exclaimed, turning around.

'Yes, thank you, I can hear that.' Evie couldn't help chuckling at his expression of horror.

'But...she's with you.'

'So?'

'So, I wouldn't have thought she'd cry with you. I thought it was just me.'

'I'm not a panacea. Once I got her changed and the nappy contortionist had left, she realised how hungry she was.'

Belatedly she realised that if she wanted to encourage him not just to look after his daughter, but actually interact more with her, then teasing him might not be the best idea. With her transplant looming all too quickly, in a couple of days she'd be in hospital; Max would be all Imogen had. But to her relief he laughed along with her.

'Glad my efforts weren't completely in vain—at

least they had entertainment value. I can't believe she was as patient as she was with me.'

'Depends on the day,' Evie responded, realising it would be good to show Max there was no magic wand. 'Some days she might be patient, other days everything might unsettle her. She's a little person, and just like you or I she has good days and off days. If things aren't going well one day, don't assume it's something you've done. There's no fix-all solution.'

Max looked even more horrified.

'If she's fed, burped, slept and has a clean nappy, she'll be happy, though, won't she?'

'Usually. Not every time. All I'm saying is don't assume you've done something wrong. Maybe it's her teeth, or growing pains, or her tummy. Just be ready just to cuddle her, that's all I do and that's what she's used to. What are you doing?'

'Getting a pen to write it down.'

'Max—' Evie was incredulous '—you're one of the foremost surgeons in your field. You said you looked after babies and young children in Gaza. You don't need to overthink it.'

'My field isn't babies. And, despite Gaza, I'm not a paediatric plastic surgeon,' he pointed out, pulling a handful of pens and an old envelope from a drawer and proceeding to test the ink.

'Also, when I do see babies in the hospital, they're usually unwell.'

She didn't mean to, but the smile erupted from her before she could hold it back. She'd never seen him anything but authoritative, completely in control of any situation or crisis, the go-to guy for several of his colleagues.

To see him so flummoxed simply by taking care of a baby, his own daughter, was something she hadn't anticipated. It somehow made him more human.

'Here, why don't you take Imogen while I get something ready for her?'

She stifled a laugh as he physically took a step backwards into the refrigerator when she advanced with the now-bawling Imogen.

'I don't think…I'm in the middle of making breakfast.'

'I can wait. Imogen won't.'

Evie held his daughter out in amusement and reluctantly he took her, delighted when Imogen's cries eased up a little. Despite his uncharacteristic uncertainty about keeping a baby happy, he was clearly more than comfortable actually holding one.

Something to do with the surgeon in him who was able to soothe and examine any patient, just as long as they weren't being asked to change nappies or feed them.

'What should I...?'

'Just cuddle her, and show her what I'm doing. Talk her through it—it might distract her.'

'Look, baby Imogen, your mummy's opening the cupboard,' he began awkwardly.

Evie stuck her head inside and laughed quietly. It was surreal watching the super-surgeon Max Van Berg so wholly out of his depth. She'd never seen it before, and she could bet no one at Silvertrees—or anywhere else, for that matter—had ever seen it, either.

'Look, your breakfast. Oh, you understood that, huh?'

She could hear his surprise as Imogen's cries lessened slightly as she turned her head to look.

'Um... Oh, I can see a breakfast bottle, how about you, Imogen?' He loosened up slightly, gaining confidence as his daughter rewarded his efforts with snuffles now instead of cries.

Evie moved around the space easily; nothing had really changed from the last time she'd been here. Except for the circumstances, of course. Max continued talking, albeit stiltedly, to his daughter until Evie was ready and offered to take Imogen back.

His relief was evident as he hurried towards her,

and she stamped down a surge of disappointment that he didn't want to feed his daughter himself. It was something she loved to do. Still, he'd made good progress. And it was only the first morning.

'What are we doing today?' Evie ventured as she settled on the chair to give Imogen her feed.

'I have surgeries this morning,' he answered apologetically.

She glanced at the clock on the wall. It was six-thirty already. He was running late.

'I cancelled all the electives I could, or passed them onto colleagues,' he answered her unspoken questions. 'I'm not on the rota for emergencies so this morning I'm clearing my desk of any immediate cases. I should be finished by the time you go in for your dialysis session this afternoon, but if not just go to the crèche and tell them who you are. They've reserved a place for Imogen until I finish.'

'Silvertrees crèche? How did you get her in there?' Evie exclaimed. 'It's a twelve-month wait list, isn't it? There was a nurse who had just put her kid down when I was working in A&E. She was told she probably wouldn't be able to get him in until he was nine months old, and she was pregnant at the time.'

'Perks of being one of Silvertrees' senior surgeons.' Max winked at her.

Her stomach flip-flopped in response.

'Isn't it just,' she murmured distractedly before a concerning thought settled on her. 'Max, you aren't planning on leaving her there every day when I go in, are you? I mean, she's never been to a crèche before. She's always had myself, or Annie. If I'd thought you weren't going to be looking after her, I would never have agreed to come here.'

'I know that, stop worrying. I told you, I have a few cases to clear off my desk but I've sorted out the rest. I've booked two weeks off and I will be looking after our daughter personally. I will not be palming her off on someone else, because I know that's what you're thinking.'

'Well, good.' She refused to apologise for caring about her daughter.

However, she didn't dare ask how he'd managed to secure two weeks off at such short notice. He'd either pulled in a fair few favours, or promised them, and she was grateful for it.

'Right, well, whilst you're feeding the baby, let me finish your breakfast.'

He passed Imogen back to her, each hand-off getting easier than the last. He was clearly growing in confidence as Imogen's father. But she needed his progress to be quicker. Max was obviously thinking of her recovery—it was one of the reasons he'd brought her here, so that she was closer to the transplant unit at Silvertrees. But she didn't know if he realised just how integral their daughter's welfare was to how stress-free her recovery would be.

Evie was determined to see some kind of bond between the two of them before she went into hospital. It would make her feel a heck of a lot more confident about being away from her precious baby girl.

CHAPTER SIX

THAT WAS THE last of the paperwork cleared up.

Max glanced at the clock on his wall in satisfaction. He was due to collect Imogen within the next half hour and take her to see Evie. Tonight might be Evie's last opportunity to spend time with her daughter before her transplant.

He had one outstanding patient, a particularly complex, long-standing case, which he intended to return to do himself. He'd already approached his colleague, Gareth Collins, to monitor the pre-op tests and pass on the results, but there were just a couple of last points he wanted to go over. Gareth was on call tonight, so Max knew if he swung by A&E he'd likely catch the guy. Hopefully in between cases.

He moved purposefully through the hospital. It was a novel experience, getting ready for time out that wasn't going to be spent out in some war zone with the charity. How was it that he had never once questioned his ability to handle anything they could throw at him, and yet the prospect of a couple of weeks with his baby daughter filled him with a long-forgotten feeling of inadequacy?

Caught up in a sudden memory of his childhood, wondering at nine years old whether he really was cut out to be a surgeon as his parents expected, he burst through the double doors only to come face to face with a familiar—battered and bloodied as usual—face.

'Hey, Dean, been fighting again?'

He crossed the resus bays to where the young boy lay, his mother worried and teary by his bedside, and his broken nose only the start of his injuries by the looks of his chart.

'Punctured lung?' He cocked his eyebrow at the kid to conceal his deep concern. 'You can't let them get to you, mate.'

Not that the boy was in much condition to respond anyway, but the soft touch didn't work with this particular lad, as Max already knew. This was the fourth time the boy had been in in as many months and the injuries were getting substantially more serious. This time it was a fractured rib with a suspected lung injury.

Max's instinct told him it had been a fight where Dean had been on the ground when he'd been kicked in his ribs. A fight Dean had likely started, from everything Max already knew.

And all because he had prominent ears. *Wing nuts. Jug-head. Dumbo.* Dean had heard them all and was desperate for surgery to correct the problem. Apparently that wasn't going to happen. Max stepped away from the curtain just as a man shot around the corner and hurtled into him.

Dean's dad.

Max caught the man before he rounded the curtain, leading him a step away.

'You know I can resolve the problem, don't you?'

'Mr Van Berg.' The man recognised him instantly.

'General anaesthetic and ten days in a bandage and it'll all be done.'

He only had to cut away the skin and tissue behind the ear and stitch the ears into their new positions. The main issue was ensuring the surgeon was competent enough to carry out a procedure that required such visual accuracy. Badly done and the patient would end up with ears that either didn't match, or looked plastered down.

Max wasn't worried. His skill wasn't in question.

'We understand.' The father nodded with a sad smile. 'But we just don't know what to do for the best. To the wife and me, Dean's a handsome little lad with a great personality, and so what if his ears stick out a little? But...'

'But...?' Max encouraged.

'But we've spoken to some experts who've said that it's just name-calling and that life can be a lot harsher than that so Dean needs to learn to ignore kids like that. They've pointed out that he can't go through life fighting everyone who says something unpleasant to him, so if we let him have surgery then he's just never going to learn how to deal with criticism.'

Easier said than done, especially when you were eleven years old. But Max appreciated Dean's parents had only their son's best interests at heart. Better than his own parents.

'And what does your gut tell you?' Max shoved away the shadows that stalked the edges of his memories.

Like the time he'd ended up in hospital for exactly the same thing at about the same age Dean was now, for pretty much the same injury. Max had had his own share of fights, and instigated by himself just like Dean. But unlike Dean, he hadn't had a valid reason for them. He hadn't got any obvious physical or mental impairment, and unlike Dean's concerned parents, who were trying to teach Dean to be strong of mind, Max could only remember his own parents expressing disappointment at such childish and *inappropriate* behaviour, before getting back to their all-important careers. But now wasn't the time to push Dean's parents.

Maybe Evie would be the best person to teach him how to go about helping the kid? He didn't know what it was but something about the boy made Max want to do more to help.

'My gut says that my son's coming home with broken bones,' the father exclaimed, torn. 'That isn't something he should have to learn to deal with at eleven years old. But I just don't know.'

'Well, you know where to find me, Mr Foster.' Max nodded. 'Any time you need me.'

Allowing the father to get back to his son, Max continued down the corridor in search of his colleague, but he couldn't shake the desire to do more for the lad. Before the kid ended up in here, and didn't leave. He'd just have to be careful; he couldn't afford to push these parents into something they weren't ready for.

By the time Max had got a moment with his busy colleague to go through the patient's notes, it had already been getting dark outside. He'd long since missed taking Imogen to see Evie, and had been compelled to call the crèche and arrange for another of his colleagues to take the baby to her mother. He'd been inflexible about being informed exactly *who* was taking his daughter, and when they were doing so, even ensuring it was a colleague he knew well. But none of it made up for the fact that he was doing the very thing he'd been so afraid of—the very reason he'd never wanted a family—he'd let them down, broken his promise to them, and all because his career had got in the way.

It had felt like small consolation that he'd subsequently swept through the hospital actively looking forward to collecting his daughter and hopefully spending a little quality time with her before putting her down in her cot.

And now, he stepped into his voluminous hallway at home, Imogen finally in his arms, as the home automation system was already lighting the house for them.

'So what shall we do, hey?' he asked his unblinking daughter.

As if in response, a pungent smell filled the air. *Wait, was that...?*

He didn't need to lift Imogen too close to his nose before he had the confirmation he needed.

'Right, little lady.' He headed quickly for the

stairs, grateful to be occupying himself. 'You definitely need a change.'

Whether she resented being taken in the opposite direction from her play mat, or simply the fact that she could sense his tenseness, her wail of objection began even before Max lowered her onto the changing mat. Pulling her legs into her tummy and trying to roll over, she made it clear that she wasn't going to make this an easy change for him.

For a moment, Max stared hopelessly. This afternoon's complex procedure had been challenging and exhilarating, but he hadn't questioned his ability for a second. So how was it that now, faced with a five-month-old baby in a dirty nappy, he was filled with self-doubt?

Ridiculous.

It might be true, but it didn't seem to make it any easier. Imogen clearly didn't trust him, which didn't make him feel any more confident.

What would Evie do?

Tentatively he lowered his head and, finding the bare skin on one flailing arm, he blew a brief raspberry. The effect was immediate as the wailing stopped. He lifted his head to let his eyes meet his daughter's. She was watching him carefully, prepared to give him a chance, but woe betide him if he moved too fast.

With a little more confidence, he blew another raspberry, on her cheek this time.

The giggle of response was heart-lifting. Max felt an unexpected surge of pride at the simple achievement of making his daughter laugh. The tentacles of a bond began to reach out between father and daughter, and as his confidence grew so too did Imogen's trust in him.

Within minutes, he had her relaxed and ready to be changed, as she happily allowed him to unbutton her Babygro and open the sticky tabs holding her nappy on.

He'd known babies' nappies smelled; he'd been around a few. But he'd never been this close to a freshly removed one before. Max wrinkled his nose in disbelief.

'That can't really have all come from you,' he teased dramatically, eliciting more giggles. 'What have they been feeding you, hey?'

He pulled a handful of wipes out of the packet, paused, then doubled it. He could hear Evie's soft chuckle of amusement in his head but he didn't care.

Then he glanced back at the nappy with concern.

'You're not coming down with something, are you?'

His head moved automatically to check her forehead, her tummy. There was no suggestion of a temperature, but still.

He'd heard of doctors—good, competent doctors—who reassured other parents about their babies every day, but who had to get colleagues to check things when they had babies of their own because they couldn't trust their own judgement. They'd always claimed it was different when it came to your own children.

He'd always thought it ridiculous. Now he wasn't so sure.

The idea of Imogen coming down with any kind of infection, especially given her additional vulnerability, actually caused his chest to tighten. The edges of a fear he'd never before experienced.

He thrust the thought away. No, the medical bit was the stuff he *could* trust; that bit he understood. Reaching for the LCD screen from the wall, Max typed in a search. Then he compared the image on the screen in front of him with the nappy. Definitely the expected colour. Imogen was fine.

And since when did he panic over nothing? Since when had he ever panicked?

Even so, it took him several minutes of carefully lifting Imogen's ankles and methodically cleaning all traces until she was perfectly pink and clean, and smelling of baby wipes, until his heart finally started to slow down. Then, dabbing a little cream in place, he deftly secured a fresh nappy in place, before lifting her up to check his handiwork.

'Pretty good.' He nodded his head at Imogen. 'We did a good job there, little lady.'

Imogen gurgled as if in agreement, then, reaching out her chubby fingers, grabbed his hair and pulled him in, giggling in anticipation of another raspberry.

'There's a rugby game on TV tonight,' he told her brightly. 'I haven't had a chance to watch a game in years. What say you grab a bottle and I'll grab a pizza, and we can watch it together?'

Imogen snuggled down into him.

'Okay, then it's agreed.' He dropped a kiss onto her head without thinking. 'I don't think this babysitting lark is going to be too bad after all.'

Although, was it really babysitting if the baby was your own? Max wondered, a half-smile moulding itself to his mouth.

Forget all his preconceptions and fears about not being a good enough father. His daughter was incredible enough to make him *learn* to become a good father. The best father he could be.

And if he was father material then surely that meant he was other kinds of family material, too?

So where might that leave him with Evie?

* * *

'How are you feeling?'

Guilty, uncertain, scared. Petrified might be more like it.

'Not bad.' She dredged up a smile.

'Good.'

'Where's Imogen?'

'Outside. One of your junior doctors jumped at the chance to cuddle her whilst I came to see if you were up to one last visit with her this morning. Apparently I'm to tell you that she's even more adorable than you made her out to be.'

'That'll be Richie.' Evie smiled again, more sincere this time. 'He's been great. He has three sisters and a brother.'

'Right.' Max nodded blankly.

'You don't know who he is, do you?'

'Should I?' Max was unconcerned. The hospital was a big place—not everyone knew each other.

'He told me he was on your service for six months a couple of years ago.'

'Come to mention it, he did look familiar,' Max responded thoughtfully, not a trace of shame at his oversight.

It was well known that Max never bothered to find out anything about the people he worked with and she knew for a fact that he'd never really considered colleagues' reasons for getting into the medical profession.

'You know, showing an interest in people's lives outside the hospital isn't always a bad thing,' she told him. 'Sometimes it reveals traits or skills you can't learn in a lecture theatre or an operating room, but which can be just as important in boosting a patient's confidence.'

'It also invites interactions with people which aren't case or hospital related,' he argued. 'And if they don't further a patient's treatment or someone's learning, then they're little more than a waste of time.'

'You sound so—' She stopped abruptly. She couldn't tell him how like his cold, unforgiving parents he sounded in that moment.

'So...what?' demanded Max harshly, as though he knew what she'd been about to say.

Wheels spun in her head.

'So jaded,' she offered, relieved when he seemed to believe her. She cleared her throat. 'Anyway, thanks for bringing Imogen back in this morning. I'll take any opportunity to spend time with her before the operation.'

'Okay, then,' he acceded, leaving her room to fetch Imogen.

Evie blew out a long breath. The transplant team

would be coming in soon to start the main pre-op process, getting her into a hospital gown, inserting an IV line into her hand and catheters in her neck to monitor her blood pressure and heart.

Her eyes pricked the moment Max rounded the corner, Imogen in his arms.

'Say hi to Mummy,' he told his daughter softly, lowering her gently into Evie's eager arms.

'Hey, sweetpea,' Evie choked out. It was illogical but being separated from her daughter, who she'd never been apart from for more than a few hours at a time since Imogen's birth, seemed like the worst part of this transplant process, so far.

As Imogen reached out, her chubby fingers locking around Evie's hair and tugging, it was frustrating to realise she didn't even have the strength to keep her daughter at bay. The previous day Imogen had been mercifully sleepy and quiet but this morning she was clearly full of energy. When Max reached out silently to take his daughter back, empathy in his gaze, Evie couldn't hold back the sob.

'Don't worry, a couple of days and it will all be different,' he soothed. 'You'll have a new kidney and you'll be strong enough for your daughter to come back and visit you again. Before you know it, your life will be better than you remember it for a long time.'

She flashed him a grateful smile, watching as he easily shifted his daughter in his arms, soothing her objections at being taken from her mother.

It was like watching a different man from the one she'd left thirty-six hours ago. Two nights alone with his daughter and already he seemed much more at ease, holding her and chatting with her. Even as he talked to Evie, he was simultaneously distracting and entertaining their baby. Not to mention the fact that Imogen was dressed beautifully, and not in a mismatch of clothes as she'd seen throughout her career when some fathers had been left in charge of their children.

'You mastered the nappy, then?' She tried for a weak joke, gratified when Max looked proud of himself.

'I have.' He grinned. 'She doesn't see me coming and shriek her head off any more.'

'You look good together,' managed Evie.

She knew she had to stay positive, stay focused, but she couldn't deny that it was a relief to know that, if anything did go wrong, Imogen would still have at least one biological parent in her life. Even though Evie knew that her brother and Annie would always be there for the little girl.

'You're not getting morbid, are you?' he chastised.

'Of course not.' Biting the inside of her cheek, Evie executed the bare-faced lie with grace. He didn't buy it for a second.

She wasn't prepared when, settling on the bed beside her, Max pulled her into his arms. She stiffened, unsure what to do. Then, like a floodgate giving way, she crumpled against him. The silent sobs wracked her body even as Max held her oblivious daughter on the other side of him, comforting her more than she could have imagined with his free hand.

He dropped a kiss onto the back of her head as she bent forward, holding onto him, her forehead resting on his chest, and she lifted her head to look at him.

'We need to talk, Max.'

'What about?' he asked her.

But now wasn't the time to tell him about his parents. Or about the money.

'Not now. If I get through this.'

'*When* you get through this,' Max corrected throatily. 'We need you, Imogen and me.'

We? The word sounded so good to her ears, even if he was only saying it to be encouraging.

For one perfect moment it was just the three of them in a bubble and nothing existed outside them. Not her transplant, not his parents, and not the fact that she and Max didn't really know the first thing about each other.

If her operation went well, then all that had to change. She and Max had to find the best solution with their daughter's best interests in mind. They needed to get to know each other. Spend time together.

Which meant she needed to tell him about his parents. And the money.

There was no more making excuses.

CHAPTER SEVEN

MAX SWEPT TOWARDS the automatic doors of the transplant unit as he had so many times before as a surgeon. But this time was different.

This whole week going backwards and forwards with Evie, even before the transplant, had been different.

He moved down to Evie's wing, pressing the buzzer for access and sanitising his hands thoroughly even though he'd done it the minute he'd dropped Imogen off at the crèche moments earlier.

'How are you?' he asked softly as he stepped into Evie's room.

'Not bad, believe it or not.'

Her voice was a little scratchy from the intubation during surgery and she was lying on the bed, awake but tired-looking. He was hardly surprised to see she was out of her hospital gown and dressed in soft, loose-fitting clothes. If she'd whipped her packed day case out of the wardrobe he wouldn't have batted an eyelid.

'The nurses warned me that you'd got yourself up and out of bed and made them help you dress the instant the anaesthetic had worn off,' he rebuked, but there was no heat in his voice.

'I've already been through this with them, Max.' Evie grinned. 'They encourage you to be active—walking reduces the swelling and expedites the recovery process. They say you should try getting up and around and into a good routine as soon as the anaesthetic wears off if you can. Certainly the day after a successful transplant, like this.'

'Which means *gradual* exercise only.' He refused to let her browbeat him the way she clearly was doing with her nurses.

'My creatinine is already down to one point four, my potassium is normal, and there're no issues from the steroids. Even the sickness is gone.' She ticked them off on her fingers as though for his benefit. 'The hardest part is remembering to drink enough water after having my fluid intake restricted for so long. Walking for my health is the least I can do.'

'Whilst still remembering what your body has just been through, and what it's trying to recover from.'

'My transplant went perfectly,' she argued.

'Your transplant went very smoothly,' he was

prepared to acknowledge. 'But that still doesn't mean you push it.'

'Fine.' She raised one hand dismissively but it was a half-hearted gesture. She was clearly tired. 'How's Imogen?'

'She's great,' he replied softly. 'But she misses you.'

All other thoughts visibly slid from Evie's head as a pain welled in her eyes, and Max felt for her. Evie obviously missed her daughter more than she'd even feared she would. It would be a while before she would be able to cuddle Imogen again, probably close to discharge. Evie was still too vulnerable to infection after her transplant, and babies like Imogen seemed to have a permanent cold or some such virus, even though Max was determined to keep Imogen as safe as he possibly could.

He determined that, after the visit was over here, he'd bring Imogen to the window outside Evie's room so that they could at least see each other, if only through the glass, as long as it didn't upset the baby. Knowing Imogen, it probably wouldn't; his daughter's resilience and strength of character was beginning to blow him away.

'She's amazing, you know.' The words tripped out of his mouth, taking both of them by surprise.

'I know.' Evie nodded vigorously.

'She's incredible, and tiny, and beautiful. And she's *my* daughter. Our daughter,' he exclaimed incredulously, pride swelling up inside him. 'I'd like to be a part of her life. A proper part.'

Time stood still as she tried to process what Max was saying. Her heart hammered in her chest.

'What do you mean by a "proper part"? How?'

'I mean that I don't want to be an occasional father.'

'So, weekends? Holidays?' There was an edge to her voice that she appeared to be unsuccessfully fighting.

'Evie?'

'I'm sorry, I don't know what's wrong with me. I always hoped you'd have a relationship with your daughter. For Imogen to have her father in her life.'

'But?' he prompted.

'Nothing,' Evie muttered, leaving him with the distinct impression there was something he was missing.

Before she could register, he reached out and took her hand in one of his, his other hand brushing a stray lock of hair from her face. He didn't understand what compelled him but it felt so oddly intimate and his chest constricted painfully.

'But how would it work, Max? Would you expect me to disrupt my life, move to be closer to you? Away from my family? The people who have supported me?'

She was trying to pick a fight with him now, he realised. He was *definitely* missing something.

'Just think about it, Evie. Okay?'

It said a lot for how he'd grown to care for Imogen in such a short time. Would Evie try to deny a relationship between them? He already knew he could never accept that. His daughter was already a part of his life. Nothing could change that.

Another awkward silence settled over them and they both shifted uncomfortably. The room was stifling. He wanted to get them both out of there, into a less claustrophobic environment, but he didn't want to strong-arm Evie.

He didn't need to worry, she must have felt the same way as she was pushing herself up and slowly swinging her legs over the side of her bed, wincing as the incision site came under pressure. He was at her side in an instant.

'Here, take my hand.'

For a moment she hesitated but then reluctantly stretched out her arm and allowed Max to help her off the bed. There they stood, toe to toe, neither of them daring to move, even daring to breathe. *Could it be that she* did *still want him, after all?*

'How do you really feel?' he asked huskily, fire practically crackling along his veins.

'It feels good to be free of the burden of dialysis, free of feeling as though my body was letting me down, free of feeling like I'm too ill to really be…attractive.'

And Max had certainly made her feel desirable with that kiss only a week ago, in that side room.

The gap between them was tiny and yet it felt like a veritable chasm. He was tempted to reach down and press his lips to hers, the way he had done a week ago, but he had no idea how she would react.

Time ticked by and still neither of them moved.

Finally, almost jerkily, Max stepped away, turning his back on her so that she couldn't read his expression. Not that he knew what it would tell her. When he spoke he heard the tell-tale hoarseness in his voice.

'Shall we go for a coffee?'

'Sure, why not?' She tried for an easy smile but it looked tight and uncomfortable on her lips and she gave up before turning away.

'Lead on, Speedy,' he tried to tease, sounding as awkward as she had.

At least that might make her feel a smidgen better.

Making her way out of the room, her body loosening up and appearing less alien with every step, she set the pace down the hallway and to the patient area. The loaded silence slowly gave way to a more companionable peace, as he'd hoped, as they left the confinement of her room behind them.

The unit had its own coffee-shop area for patients. Larger, well-ventilated and more voluminous than anywhere in the main hospital, and off limits to anyone not in the transplant suite, the coffee shop was somewhere post-op patients could go without being exposed to any number of coughs, colds or other bugs.

Settling into a comfy chair without argument, she let him get the drinks and bring them over. Then he selected a sturdy-looking round tub chair opposite her and folded one ankle over his opposite knee before taking a casual sip of the hot drink.

She dragged her eyes up from his thighs and eyed his coffee enviously before casting a reproachful gaze at the glass of cool, filtered water he had handed her.

'Drink it,' he commanded, not unkindly. 'Your fluid input will be noted on your chart later.'

'Thanks for that.'

But at least it raised a weak smile. Max relaxed. They would get there. Together they would find a harmonious balance and, by the time Evie was cleared for discharge, they would know what they were going to do for their daughter's future.

'I can't believe she crashed like that.' Evie sighed as he headed back down the stairs, having put Imogen into her cot for the first night home since the transplant.

'I can.' Max chuckled from the hallway. 'The excitement at seeing you home again wiped her out. Snatching a couple of hours with you morning and evening hasn't been the same as finally having her mummy home.'

Evie swelled with pride, and Max marvelled at how far the two of them had come since that first day post-op in the hospital. It was hard to believe that was a week ago already. He had visited religiously, bringing Imogen to the window so that Evie could see her daughter and talk to her through the opening. And then Imogen had been able to come in to visit her, and he'd done everything he could to ensure he didn't take his daughter anywhere she could pick up any bugs to pass on to Evie.

Evie. She looked beautiful, and vivacious, and exhausted. He should pack her off to bed.

Alone.

Whilst he did something to distract himself from the fact that as their friendship had burgeoned over the last week, so too had his reviving feelings for Evie. Which was going to be the last thing she wanted to hear from him.

Hence his need for a distraction. Like watching some mindless film on TV.

Although, given Evie's reaction to him in the hospital corridor when they'd first bumped into each other a couple of weeks ago, it was patent that there were still *some* residual feelings of their former attraction to one other. But was it purely sexual chemistry, or was there something more?

And as much as he wanted Evie, could happily take her to bed right now, he knew he couldn't. It would never be the fun, no-strings fling of last year. They had a daughter together and they still needed to work out the best solution for her future, without complicating things unnecessarily.

And yet, sex was all he could guarantee. He was still the same man he'd been beforehand, still committed to his career, unable to risk splitting his focus. He couldn't give either Evie or Imogen the family life they would get closer to their own family.

So he wanted her, he could admit that. He wanted her in the most primal way. But the difference was that he was evolved, and this was one base need he was going to have to overrule.

'Anyway...' he pushed aside all his concerns, as he had been doing for the last ten days '...a good, peaceful night's sleep—for both of you—and you'll be ready for more time together tomorrow.'

'I *am* pretty beat,' Evie conceded reluctantly.

'So get some sleep.'

'I can't.' She shook her head. 'I mean, I know I won't be able to drop off. My mind is still racing and I'll just lie there staring at the clock if I go now.'

Yeah, he could relate to that.

'I thought I might watch a film or something. You want to join me?' she offered.

'A film?' he echoed sharply.

So much for his idea of distracting himself. They'd watched a few films together during their brief fling. After all, they'd needed some rest and refuelling—as incredible as the sex had been, even they hadn't managed it twenty-four hours a day. That said, their film watching had inevitably ended only one way.

'Why not?' She shrugged nonchalantly, her brain apparently not in the same gutter as his. 'I could just do with a bit of relaxing with some mindless entertainment.'

He resisted the urge to make a wry quip.

'Okay, let's watch a film together.'

'You choose one. I just want to change...'

'Into something more comfortable?' he teased, the cliché slipping out before he could swallow it down. 'That is, more comfortable over the incision site?'

He cringed internally. He'd had no intention of revealing to Evie just how fragile his control over himself was right now. Thankfully, she seemed too preoccupied with her own thoughts to notice.

'Right,' she muttered. 'My wound.'

'Okay. Meet you in there when you're ready.' He retreated into the kitchen for something to eat.

He wasn't even that hungry but he felt the need to occupy his hands if nothing else. His mind trying to put the brakes on the X-rated thoughts going on in the background, Max yanked the cupboards open with unnecessary vigour.

A bag of microwavable popcorn. That would do.

By the time he returned to the lounge Evie was gliding in, dressed in a light grey jersey pyjama-style tracksuit. He tried not to look her up and down, but it was impossible. The clothes emphasised long, slender legs, which had once wrapped so tightly around his hips, a slim waist he had held with his palms and, as the light material clung to the contours of breasts he could picture whenever he closed his eyes, his fingers itched to pull down the zip to reveal more than just that delicious glimpse of cleavage on offer right now.

So much for his desire for self-control.

He tried not to remember the sweet hollow spot at the base of her neck, which was on clear view now as Evie's long hair was pulled up into a sleek ponytail. She unselfconsciously reached for a handful of popcorn, oblivious to the less than pure thoughts running through his head right now.

He seriously needed to pull himself together.

'All set.' He gave a long-forgotten *just friends* smile and gestured to the home control pad in his hands as if that clarified things. Selecting the movie, he commanded the home system to dim the lights just as Evie held out the bowl.

'Popcorn?'

As she moved a familiar gentle perfume, essentially Evie scent, reached his nostrils. In an instant, his jeans grew taut over his groin. Odd, how the olfactory sense was so powerful it could evoke the most vivid of images. Not least right now when he had a flashback to Evie, wild and abandoned in his bed as he grazed his teeth over the sensitive skin just below her ear. And the added low lighting certainly wasn't helping matters.

Grateful for the proffered snack food, he grasped the bowl and rammed it almost painfully down into his lap.

Since when had he turned into a horny, fifteen-year-old adolescent? He had a feeling he wasn't going to remember much of this film, after all.

CHAPTER EIGHT

EVIE WOKE UP and lay for a moment in the darkness, trying to get her bearings.

She was back in Max's home. And after last night, living here with Max felt even more loaded with frustrated longing than before she'd gone in to hospital.

The whole week, ever since that moment when she'd been scared before the transplant and Max had reassured her, she'd felt the old feelings resurfacing with a vengeance. And feeling her whole body change, almost overnight, when Annie's kidney had begun to clear out her body naturally, Evie had realised there was no more dialysis, no more feeling sluggish, no more telling herself how unattractive she was, no more missing out on the fun things because she was lacking in basic energy.

Her whole life was going to improve, something she hadn't dared hope before. Her relationship with Imogen was going to be so much better now she had more strength and energy. And her relationship with Max was blossoming as she felt her former confidence returning.

Yet last night…well, what had happened last night?

She didn't remember a single second of the film; she'd been too busy being hyper-aware of every move Max had made. She'd been sure she hadn't misread the signals; that they both felt the attraction, and she'd been equally sure that, given half a chance, they could revisit something of their fling last year.

By contrast, Max had been absorbed in the film, and oblivious of her more X-rated thoughts. Hardly the greatest ego-boost she could have hoped for. She didn't know how she'd got it all so wrong, but the humiliation still stung her cheeks whenever she thought about it.

So right now she really needed a release mechanism. A brisk walk on the treadmill in Max's gym would not only meet the daily exercise goals of her post-op recovery, but it would help to expend some of her pent-up energy.

Maybe.

At least the gym being in the basement meant that she wouldn't wake either Max or Imogen. Although with its high-level windows allowing plenty of natural light, it had never felt like a claustrophobic space to her, plus it was well-ventilated enough to more than satisfy her transplant requirements.

Easing herself carefully out of bed, Evie dressed quickly, only struggling to put her socks and trainers on, and then crept quietly out of the master suite and down to the basement.

The last person she expected to see was Max.

A hot and sweaty Max.

She hovered in the doorway and wondered if he'd seen her or if she could discreetly back away.

'Are you coming in, then?' he asked.

Clearly not the latter, then.

Evie scanned the room. A towel was hung over the treadmill and weights were scattered around his bench; he'd clearly been here a while. He looked pumped, slick, and impressively fit.

Of course he did.

'Um, I was after the treadmill, but you're obviously busy. I can come back later.'

'No need.' Max sprang up with enviable energy and ducked across the room to retrieve his towel. 'I finished on there before. I just have a few reps here and I'll be out of your hair if you prefer.'

'No, no, that's fine.'

It wasn't really. She didn't need Max seeing her pathetic attempt to walk a couple of miles whilst he knocked out reps like some elite athlete.

'I couldn't sleep,' she offered, willing her feet to move. After some objection, they mercifully obeyed.

'Me neither. But our daughter is gently snoring her little head off.'

He jerked his head and a baby monitor blinked at her from the small side table. So it wasn't Imogen keeping him awake, then.

'Has she been asleep all this time?'

'No chance. I think the excitement of seeing you home last night got to her.'

Evie smiled warmly. Their reunion, as brief as it had been and given Imogen understood so little, had been the most uplifting experience she could have imagined.

'Just as we suspected, her tummy woke her in the night and she had a good feed and a little play. So she'll probably sleep longer than usual this morning.'

'Oh, right.'

She wanted her daughter to rest, but she was longing to cuddle the little girl again.

And as for Max—did it make things better or worse that it was just overtiredness keeping him awake? For one brief moment she had allowed herself to think it might be the same sexual frustration that she'd been feeling, that maybe last night hadn't been as easy for him as she'd believed. But she'd only been fooling herself.

Stepping onto the treadmill, Evie started off her mid-speed walk and tried to concentrate on the low-level music.

Don't look.

At least she was getting fitter and stronger every day.

Think of anything else but the fact that he doesn't even have a shirt on.

And soon she would be back to normal.

And what else?

Then she could take Imogen back to Annie's.

Nope, it was an exercise in futility.

Her eyes snapped inexorably back to Max. She hungrily drank in the sight of his body rippling and pumping oh-so-deliciously as his muscles worked in exquisite harmony. She had no idea she'd been effectively ogling for a good twenty minutes until he wound up his reps and she glanced at the screen on the treadmill.

'So, how are you going?' he asked, sauntering casually over once he'd cleared his weights away.

She was only grateful she hadn't chosen to wear a heart monitor. It would be bleeping like crazy right about now, and it had nothing to do with how hard she was pushing herself in an attempt to drown out her lamenting libido.

'Not too bad.' She breathed out hard.

Max frowned.

'Are you sure that isn't too fast?'

'Brisk,' she countered. 'That's the key. Once I've got over the first few weeks, I can probably start on a bike, or the cross trainer.'

'Fine, I'll show you how to use that one over there when you're ready. It's not the most user-friendly model I could have chosen.' Max slotted his water bottle into the holder on her machine. 'Here, drink this.'

Evie didn't answer. Did he really expect her to still be here in a few weeks' time? Wouldn't he be expecting her to leave soon?

'Okay, I'm going to leave you to it. Imogen will be waking soon and I wouldn't mind a shower before the nappy changes and feeding begin.' He chuckled.

He was trying, but they were both aware how stilted the conversation was.

'Good idea.'

'Everything okay?'

How was it he could read her so easily?

'I'm just a bit tired, that's all,' she lied, hating the fact that she was using the transplant as an excuse but not wanting him to guess at the real reason for her distraction.

Evie waited, only releasing her breath as he dipped his head in a curt nod, then left the room. She threw herself into her walking for the next twenty minutes, but once the timer ended she still wasn't ready to return upstairs. Everywhere she went in this house had X-rated memories haunting every inch of her brain. Selecting a harder, longer, uphill programme, Evie was determined to clear her mind of everything but getting better.

By the time she finished the second exercise programme and left the home gym to climb the first set of stairs from the basement, she already knew she'd pushed too hard. Every muscle ached. The last thing she needed was to collide with the rock-solid, Max-shaped wall with an undignified *oomph*.

'What the…? Have you been in the gym all this time?' he demanded angrily. 'No, don't answer that, I can see it for myself. You're practically white, Evie.'

'I think I did a bit too much,' she admitted quietly, wondering if she was going to be sick or whether she just *thought* she was going to be.

'You think?'

'I just… *Hey!*' She panicked as he scooped her

up into his arms. 'I need a shower—what are you doing?'

'I'm doing exactly what it looks like. I'm carrying you into the kitchen because, frankly, you're never going to make it upstairs by yourself, and I think you could do with something inside your stomach. Your shower can wait, unless you want to risk collapsing?'

'You're right,' Evie answered slowly, trying to ignore the way every nerve ending in her body felt it was on fire beneath Max's touch. 'I think I probably am a bit hungry.'

At least her stomach didn't let her down, giving a thunderous rumble of agreement at the mention of food.

She wasn't quite prepared for the indignity of Max instructing her to peel off her damp tee shirt and handing her his warm fleece jacket. Not even the sight of her in her bra caused a raised eyebrow from him, she thought glumly. A far cry from the fervour with which they had repeatedly devoured each other a year ago.

But within moments she was seated on a chair, a mouth-watering glass of no-longer-forbidden orange juice in front of her, Imogen in her line of sight and playing happily with some soft blocks, whilst Max whisked up two omelettes.

Evie watched in silence considering how, to an outsider, it might have looked like a scene of blissful domesticity. How wrong they would be. She pushed the thought from her head, wondering why she felt so down. But last night had only proved that whatever attraction had once bounced between her and Max, it was now gone. At least, on his part. So she might as well just enjoy the here and now with him as the father of her child, if nothing else.

'D'you know I haven't been able to eat a whole-egg omelette for almost a year?' She forced herself to smile, realising that it wasn't all that difficult as Max set the warm plate down in front of her and slipped into the far seat so that he didn't block her view of their daughter.

'Well, I make a mean omelette if I say so myself. Plus there's a bagel with cream cheese and some smoked salmon if you want it.'

'You remembered.' She was surprised. Not that she could eat all that now, but it had been her favourite breakfast when working in the hospital, and Max had made it for her a couple of mornings during their fling. When they'd dragged themselves out of bed, that was. Or the shower. Or the swivel office chair.

They ate in companionable silence before Evie reluctantly pushed her chair back, carrying her plate over to the worktop.

'Thanks,' she told him sincerely. 'I guess I'd better go and get a shower before the sweat dries on me and I get a chill. Can't imagine Professor Goodwin would be amused.'

'Not really,' Max agreed. 'Leave that, I'll sort it.'

Pivoting on her heel as best she could, Evie headed upstairs, finally allowing herself the indulgence of breathing in Max's unique scent from his fleece. A bittersweet sensation, which brought back memories of their time together, as well as a sadness that it would never be like that between them again. And there wasn't a damn thing she could do about it.

At least the shower in her bathroom called seductively to her and, after checking her blood pressure and temperature were within the expected ranges, Evie headed into the tiled area, the underfloor heating making the floor as pleasant to walk over as she remembered.

'*Hello*, power shower,' she murmured, looking at the oversized walk-in shower she had fallen in love with in those few days before going into hospital.

Turning the chrome-spoked wheel and selecting the waterfall setting, Evie stepped back and flashed a triumphant smile as the steaming-hot water spilled out. Now all she had to do was strip off.

Easier said than done.

It took her almost five minutes to divest herself of her exercise outfit. Stretching still pulled at the incision, especially after having overdone it in the gym, and she didn't want to give the wound any reason to seep and not heal perfectly.

She was in the uncomfortable process of twisting her arms back to try to reach her bra clips when she realised she wasn't going to be able to lift her arms high enough to wash her hair. Not a pleasant prospect given the way she'd sweated in the gym, trying to empty her mind of wanton thoughts of Max. Evie stopped, leaning on the marble countertop as she tried to decide the best course of action.

Leave it. Or ask Max for help.

She chewed on her lip nervously.

What was a realistic solution? She really couldn't afford *not* to wash her hair, but she could hardly bend double over the sink—her body wasn't quite recovered for that yet. Short of getting into the shower with her, how was Max supposed to help her? She froze at the images that conjured. Not least the memories of the shower they'd shared during their nights together. She could almost feel the water coursing over her skin as Max had explored her with his mouth.

Stop right there, she warned herself silently. If the way he'd divested her of her top downstairs was anything to go by, he'd be professional, polite and not in the least bit attracted to her. She'd do well to follow his lead, and if he could be detached then so could she.

Besides, there was nothing else for it.

Slamming off the shower and snatching up a towel, she squared her shoulders and went in search of Max. Grateful to see him coming up the stairs as she reached the landing.

'I need your help,' she announced without preamble. 'Please?'

She didn't dare look over her shoulder to check he was following her as she marched back into the bathroom, grateful for the steam, which offered at least the psychological semblance of privacy.

Professional, polite, detached. Professional, polite, detached... She repeated it like a mantra so by the time she faced Max she was more composed than she'd been before.

'You want my help…for a shower?'

He sounded aghast but she refused to let it get to her.

Professional, polite, detached. She could do it. She would do it.

'To wash my hair,' she explained. 'We can keep underwear on—it'll be like a bikini for the beach.'

Well, no, not really, but she could pretend that was what she was thinking.

'This is ridiculous,' he muttered, shaking his head and walking out of the bathroom without another word. Evie watched the empty doorway and tried to quash the sense of loss.

The minutes ticked by, and still Max didn't return. *Talk about adding insult to injury.* He wasn't attracted to her yet the idea of stepping into the shower had appalled him that much, he wouldn't even entertain helping her. It was a sobering realisation.

Did it matter if ten other men found her attractive in the future? Wouldn't she always remember that the one man who really counted, at least in her head, had been so shamefully turned off by her?

There was nothing else she could do. She would just have to try her best to do it alone. With a shake of her head, she resumed her attempts to unhook her bra.

'You've done your obs?'

Evie swung around, dropping her arms too late

and folding them across her chest as he reappeared in the doorway, the baby monitor in his hand.

'*That* was where you went? To check on our daughter?'

'Where else?' he managed, surprised at the relief in her tone. Where had she thought he'd gone? 'You didn't answer me, though. Have you done your obs?'

'I have,' she confirmed awkwardly. 'How's Imogen?'

'She's asleep. Like I said, long night teething and she didn't sleep in as long as I'd expected this morning. She just wanted a bit of a play and some breakfast of her own to fill her little tum and she was ready for a catch-up nap.'

His gaze dropped to her chest as it peeked out from behind her forearms.

'So, do you need some help?'

'No,' she squeaked, coughing to regain her normal voice. 'I'm fine now.'

A beat passed.

'Clearly you're struggling.' Max blew out a breath and walked back into the room. 'Turn around.'

'No, I'm fine. I just…'

'Quit stalling and turn around, Evie.'

He had to stay composed, not give away just how much she still turned him on. He'd managed it downstairs in the kitchen when he'd got her to strip off her wet top, though it had taken some effort. He just had to remember that she wouldn't recover if she wasn't relaxed, which meant not making her feel uncomfortable, as though he might pounce on her any second.

He had to think of her like any other patient. He was never attracted to them no matter how attractive they were.

Except that she wasn't any other patient. She was Evie. And that was what made her stand out from anyone else he'd ever known.

The heavy silence hung between them as Max reached around and unhooked her bra in one simple, efficient movement.

'Hey!' she gulped.

'How did you get it on?' he asked.

'Sorry?'

He cocked an eyebrow at her.

'How did you get the bra on? If you can't get it off?'

'I put it on forwards and turned it around.' She flushed prettily. 'But, like you said, I did a bit too much this morning and my muscles have already started to tighten up.'

'So, do you need help with your briefs, or can you do that?'

'They stay on. And you can hook my bra back on, too. Like a bikini, remember?'

'Evie, I'm supposed to be here to help you. I'm a surgeon, and we're both adults. I'm sure we can see this for what it is and control ourselves.'

Why did that sound like a challenge to himself? Still, he'd always relished a challenge.

Deftly he slid the item from behind her towel and slung it into the wicker laundry basket without even turning round. The corners of her mouth twitched despite her nerves.

'Fluke,' she teased him unexpectedly.

He stuffed down the flare of attraction.

'Entirely,' he agreed. 'Now, get in the shower.'

They were dancing dangerously close to the flames, he thought as he shed his own clothing, watching her silhouette through the steamed-up glass panel of the shower. He had no idea what he thought he was doing, agreeing to wash her hair like this, but he hadn't been able to stop himself. The fact that his body was already reacting to the shadowy pink silhouette wasn't filling him with hope, but he could hardly change his mind now. Stripping down to his boxers, Max dumped everything in the laundry basket, schooled his thoughts and picked up her shampoo and conditioner before stepping into the shower. An all too familiar, soft, perfect backside drew his gaze and his body tightened further. He was going to have to keep his distance.

Quickly, he stretched his arm around Evie to place the bottles on the marble-tiled alcove, making a conscious effort to avoid contact with her skin. Then, picking the shampoo bottle back up and squeezing out a generous amount for her long hair, he lathered it onto her scalp. As he worked his way through, he watched her place her fingers on the alcove to brace herself and gave a satisfied nod. She wasn't as strong as she liked to make out; her body was still recovering and this shower would have been too much for her alone. With a renewed sense of vindication, Max concentrated on sectioning out her hair and shampooing.

Despite their wildly insatiable desire for each other last year, it was this simple activity that felt the most intimate to Max. Something that people having a basic fling would never do for each other. A quietly affectionate gesture, to wash her hair like this.

He rather liked it.

It was only when the first few strands began to come away that he realised what was happening. It wasn't a lot, but temporary hair loss or breakage was one of the known side effects of some of the medications Evie was taking, until the nephrology team had chance to balance her doses. Max contemplated whether or not to mention it to her now. She would already be aware of the probability, but did she really need the added stress of it actually happening now? And to his mind, it didn't make her any less attractive, or any less of a woman.

He finished shampooing her hair and gently leaned her to one side so that as he rinsed her hair the suds didn't run down on the incision side of her body. Then he started all over again with the conditioner.

Finally, his task complete and his body reined in, Max reached for the tortoiseshell clip he knew she used, twisted her hair up and tied it back. It wasn't exactly neat, but it would do, and it kept her hair from sweeping across her back and dripping any residual hair product near her wound.

His eyes swept over the smooth skin of her back, which his hands remembered so well.

'Here.' His voice was gruffer than he'd intended. 'I'll do your back since you can't reach it.'

She froze momentarily before relinquishing the body puff to him. Swiftly, he soaped her shoulders and back then over her sides, taking care not to linger or to go too close to the wound. Eventually he felt Evie begin to relax. He worked his way downwards using circular movements, covering the backside that was causing his body such difficulties, and bending down to cover the backs of her legs.

There. Done. Give her the body puff back and stand up.

Slowly, almost against his own will, his hands reached up to her waist, his head in line with her hips as he angled her slightly towards him, ignoring her initial resistance, still using the body puff to lather the hip closest to him. He turned her more until his face was inches away from the apex of her thighs.

He could recall the way she tasted, the way she felt. His body tightened in response and he moved the body puff across her abdomen as if to remind himself of what he was supposed to be doing. He inched up, his eyes now level with her incision, her hand hovering over it as if to hide it from him.

'Let me check it?' Half-question, half-command.

She paused, before slowly moving her arm.

Max inspected it. It was healing well.

'Looks good,' he concluded, glancing up at her.

Evie's face was flushed, embarrassed, her eyes closed and her head turned slightly away, as though she didn't dare look at him.

As though she was ashamed of him seeing her

scar. As though she was ashamed of the new soft-ness around her abdomen after carrying their daughter, he realised incredulously.

Max ran a hand down over her belly, her flinch-ing confirming his suspicions.

He opened his mouth to tell her not to be em-barrassed, that they were a symbol of how strong she was, after all she'd been through this year. But then he realised she wouldn't believe him. Still, he didn't need to say anything; actions spoke louder than words, right?

He dropped his gaze to the full breasts that his hands ached to touch. The perfect brown nipple he longed to take in his mouth. Before he could stop himself, with one hand still on her hip, his other hand trailed up the opposite side of her body to her ribcage, the underside of her breasts. He left it there whilst he placed a kiss on her belly.

She moved one hand to hide the skin but didn't push him away.

'If this is about your scar or your body, I don't want to hear it,' he growled. 'But if you really want me to stop, you say so now and I will.'

The wait almost killed him, but she said nothing as her breathing shallowed and the underside of her breast skimmed his knuckles. It was the sig-nal he needed.

He flicked out the thumb to caress her nipple and, despite the hot shower, Evie's skin goosebumped instantly in response, a low sound escaping her lips. He hardened immediately, straightening up until he could replace his thumb with his tongue, revelling in the way Evie slipped her fingers through his hair without any more hesitation, her other hand on his shoulder. He drew the hard nipple into his mouth, his tongue playing with it, his hands roaming the satiny skin of her body as she gripped his shoulder harder, arching slightly against him.

'Kiss me, Max.'

The instruction was shaky but it was there, and Max slowly straightened up, his mouth claiming hers in one movement. Still, he was only too happy to oblige when she took his hand and returned it to its earlier ministrations of her breast, her own hand reaching for him as she gave a small sound of pleasure when he flexed in her palm.

Her hand closed around him, exactly the way she knew would get him, and he groaned with need, wanting to touch her, taste her, fill her. He stepped back to give his hand room to reach down between her legs, but as he removed his support from her she swayed and stumbled.

What the hell was he doing, pushing her like that?

Evie was still recovering. She might be trying

to act as though she were recovering quickly but that didn't mean she was ready for this no matter how she'd reacted. He should have known better than to act on it. He was supposed to be taking care of her, looking out for her. Not giving in to his desire for her.

Drawing away, he reached for the taps and spun them closed. Then, grabbing a bath sheet from the towel rail, he bundled Evie up and lifted her into his arms.

'Max, what are you doing?'

Wordlessly, he carried her through to the bedroom and lowered her gently onto the master bed, before leaving the room. He needed to get to work and start his day. And maybe a couple of nights on call at the hospital would be the best thing for both Evie and himself, too.

CHAPTER NINE

PULLING THE CAR into the garage, Max leaned back in his seat and rubbed his hand over his neck. It had taken three days of gruelling surgeries, just to keep himself busy, sleeping at the hospital, and stop any wayward thoughts of Evie.

He didn't know how to even begin to apologise to her for pushing her the other morning in the shower, his desire for her overwhelming his sense of what was right. He doubted she would be happy to see him this morning. He would have stayed away longer if he could and afforded her more space, but she had a post-op check-up in a couple of hours and he needed to ensure she didn't miss it and was recovering well.

Despite everything, an inner peace had descended on him the moment the garage door had closed neatly behind him and he'd turned the engine off.

Home.

Sliding out of the car, he walked quietly through

the connecting door to the hallway, careful not to make too much noise, which could wake Evie or Imogen, when a shadowy shape flickered in his peripheral vision.

'What the...?'

Sidestepping the figure as it suddenly advanced towards him, he snapped the light on and spun around. A white-faced Evie blinked back at him, the loft hatch stick gripped in tight knuckles like a cricket bat. Her shoulders sagged slightly as she realised it was him.

She looked fierce, and frightened, and adorable. He tried to stop his lips from twitching.

'I didn't mean to scare you, sorry.'

'Where the heck have you been?'

The anger in her tone was undeniable and Max's heart sank. If he'd held out any faint hopes that she might have forgiven him his indiscretion with her, then he knew now that wasn't going to happen. He couldn't blame her, but still it cut him to think that she was that furious with him. That he'd betrayed her trust so irrevocably.

So much for the friendship truce he'd promised her a week earlier. He had to tackle it head-on, before she could say anything to make him feel worse than he already did.

'Evie, I'm sorry about the other day. It shouldn't

have happened. It was a serious misstep on my part and one which I can assure you will never happen again.'

'A misstep?' She narrowed her eyes at him and his brain whirred.

Was calling it a misstep too flimsy? Dismissing it as less important than it really was?

'A mistake,' he stated flatly, thrusting aside the voice that argued it hadn't felt like a mistake at the time. It had felt natural, and right, as if the two of them fitted together.

What was wrong with him? He felt his face twist into a sneer. Clearly Evie didn't share his rosy version of events or he wouldn't have felt it best to stay away until now.

'A dreadful mistake,' he emphasised. 'For which I am entirely to blame.'

'Oh.'

She sounded less than impressed.

'Anyway, what's all this?' He reached over to prise the long loft-hatch pole from her fingers, hoping in vain to lighten the atmosphere.

'I was frightened you might be a burglar,' she snapped coldly, pursing her lips.

'And you thought you'd come down here and confront them? With a thin stick of wood that would shatter as soon as it made contact with something hard, like a human skull?'

'It was all I could find quickly.' She eyed him defiantly.

'You seriously thought you could cause damage with this thing? You know the house is armed to the nth degree, right?' he rebuked gently. 'If I really *had* been an intruder, you should have stayed upstairs, locked the doors and called the police.'

'And let them come and get us? No chance,' spluttered Evie. 'Although you really need to have a rounders bat or a cricket bat hanging around. That would have been a lot better.'

'You didn't think that it might just be me?' He chanced another attempt at coaxing her out of her fury. 'It *is* my house.'

'Apparently so,' Evie ground out, furiously refusing to be placated. 'Yet you abandoned me here.'

'Abandoned?' he scoffed. 'That's a bit overdramatic, surely?'

'Abandoned,' Evie repeated angrily. 'You beat a hasty retreat to your safe haven of the hospital the minute things got a little...*muddied* here. It didn't exactly fit with you dragging me from the security of my family with the claim that my recovery here would be better than it would have been with them.'

Max folded his arms across his chest, ready to argue with her, before realising she had a valid point. Or, more accurately, another valid point. He *had* wrestled her from her brother's house claiming he would take care of her and Imogen. And he *had* left her alone when he'd come on so strong. But he'd assumed that would be what she wanted.

'I thought you'd prefer some space,' he managed, less certainly now.

'You left me here, with no word as to where you were or how long you'd be there. When you'd return here, *if* you'd return here. I have no one I know around me, and it was just Imogen and I for the last few days. And you think I preferred that?'

She spat the accusation at him as he stood, dumbfounded.

'You knew I was at the hospital, though. And I asked Edina to make sure you were okay.'

'Oh, yes, your cleaning lady. Thanks for your concern,' Evie choked out sarcastically.

Max hesitated. He *had* been concerned. More than he'd cared to admit. But he'd thought Edina was the most neutral party to check Evie's welfare.

'After…what happened, I assumed you'd prefer me not to be around for a while.'

Evie opened her mouth, then blew out hard.

'You assumed wrong,' came her eventual clipped

response. 'It's quiet here. And lonely. I'm used to the bustle of family. You should have asked me, checked with me.'

'You're right,' Max acknowledged.

She was hurt, he realised with a jolt.

It was an eye-opener. He'd expected Evie to be furious with him for coming back so soon. But he hadn't considered she might be hurt that he'd left her alone in the first place. *Abandoned* her, as she'd put it.

She didn't even seem to care about what had happened that night before he'd left, apart from her initial dislike of him dismissing it as merely a misstep.

'Do you want a coffee?' he asked gently. 'A tea?'

'Geez, Max,' she grumbled, but the initial heat had dissipated from her voice. 'It's so early it's still practically the middle of the night. I'm going back to bed.'

'Right.' He swallowed abruptly as she stomped back up the stairs and he noticed her attire for the first time. A strappy vest did a poor job of covering generous curves, whilst light pyjama bottoms followed the contours of her bottom.

He dragged his gaze away but the heat was already suffusing his body.

He was in serious trouble. One tiny indication

that she might not be as immune to him as he'd first thought and his resolve was crumbling again, faster than a chocolate sunbed on a sunny beach.

This was shaping up to be more of a roller coaster than their fling had been, and all he could hope to do was hold on and see where the ride took him.

'So, that brings us to section six: *Sex after transplantation.*'

A low groan of objection escaped Evie's lips and she shifted uncomfortably in the consultant's office chair.

After her humiliation of the other day, and their cringeworthy row earlier this morning, the last thing she wanted to do was to discuss the intimate details of her libido whilst sitting a foot away from the man who stirred said libido but who couldn't have been less attracted to her.

'I really don't think we need to go into that now.'

Undaunted by her lack of enthusiasm, however, her nephrologist shot her a smile as she slid a pamphlet across the coffee table separating them.

'Evie.' Arabella Goodwin cocked an eyebrow at her. 'We're all adults here and, whilst I appreciate you and Max kept your relationship impressively discreet whilst you were working between here and the centre, we do nevertheless need to consider the fact that you clearly have a healthy sexual relationship.'

'Oh…no…we don't…that is, there is no…relationship.'

'I do understand you don't want to be part of the rumour mill, Evie,' the woman cut in, not unkindly, 'but I also understand that you have a daughter together, and therefore we really do need to cover this material as part of your post-operative care. However, please rest assured that nothing said in here will leave my office.'

'No…it's just…' Evie tried again, her cheeks stinging with humiliation as she felt unusually flustered. She wanted to look to Max for support but was concerned that he might not wish to be dragged further into it. Besides, she couldn't bring herself to meet his gaze. As a doctor she might have asked similar kinds of personal questions without thinking twice, but it was very different from discussing her own sex-life with former colleagues. And, again, there was that little issue of doing so in front of Max.

As if reading her mind, Max shifted in his own seat and cleared his throat calmly. She waited for his icy tone to set his colleague straight once and for all.

'Please, Arabella.' His voice was controlled, polite. 'As you say, we kept things discreet when we were colleagues but, yes, we have a daughter together. Do continue.'

With a squeak of embarrassment Evie snatched her hand away from the pamphlet.

She snapped her head around, no longer too ashamed to look him in the face, only to be met with his steely gaze. Clearly he wasn't encouraging—what threatened to be a deeply intimate—conversation for his own entertainment or to make her feel any more humiliated than she already did. But his expression was unreadable. She was going to have to go along with it, for now, but she made a mental note to challenge him just as soon as they were alone again.

Not that *that* was a particularly thrilling prospect at this moment, either.

'Thank you. Let's start by noting that there are many factors which can influence sexual desire after transplantation, not least a patient's self-confidence.'

With a *whoosh* of breath, Evie resigned herself to the inevitable conversation, which already had her feeling as uncomfortable as she had when, as a teenager, she had been caught with her boyfriend at the time by her bumbling stepfather, who had subsequently attempted to have *The Talk*. She reached subconsciously once more for the pamphlet as Professor Goodwin continued.

'During the pre-operative period, especially when on dialysis, there are obviously more toxins around the body, which might have influenced your physical health. But also going through the process of dialysis could understandably have made you feel less confident in yourself?'

There was an expectant lull and Evie realised with a start that she was expected to offer her personal experience here.

Oh, joy.

She cast a surreptitious glance at Max, but he was steadfastly ignoring her, focused on the nephrologist. She twisted the pamphlet in her hands, buying herself a few more precious moments. With her palms sweating she felt more like an adolescent than a woman, and a doctor to boot.

'It's not exactly the...sexiest thing, being on dialysis, is it?' she mumbled.

'So you experienced a loss of sex drive?'

Her whole face felt as though it were on fire. This was excruciating. How many times had she replayed their wild, sensual explosive five nights together, just to get through the last year?

'Not exactly a loss, no.'

Both Max and the surgeon sat—one waiting

stiffly, the other waiting patiently—for her to carry on. Clearly they weren't about to let her off the hook. She saw Professor Goodwin, glancing down at her lap, pucker her eyebrows. Following the surgeon's eyes, Evie finally noticed the shredded pamphlet on her own lap.

Giveaway or what?

'I know this isn't the easiest conversation to have, Evie. But understanding what point you're at both mentally and physically, in terms of your sexual needs, is an important part of the recovery process. Which is why it helps to acknowledge where you were before the transplant and where you hope to be post-transplant, as your recovery progresses.'

Evie jerked her head into something resembling a nod, working her tongue into a response.

'It was a difficult year,' she started, falteringly. 'My renal deterioration was quite rapid, especially being pregnant with Imogen, and I went from feeling completely healthy eighteen months ago, to needing dialysis five times a week during the last few months of carrying Imogen.'

'So which do you believe had the greater impact on your sex drive? The physical drain of the pregnancy and dialysis, or the psychological effect of them?'

'I don't know.' Evie tapped out some unknown tune on the wood as she stalled for time. 'A bit of both, I suppose.'

'And can you remember…? When was the last time you wanted physical intimacy?'

This was the question she'd most wanted to avoid. Especially here, in front of Max. A fresh wave of heat flooded her cheeks, but what choice did she have?

'A few days ago,' she muttered awkwardly.

She felt Max's eyes burning into her neck, and kept her gaze resolutely forward.

'Hmm, you're currently…' Professor Goodwin checked her notes '…eleven days post-op, so that's very positive. And did you actually have physical intimacy?'

Evie shook her head.

'Was that because of a lack of energy? Because the desire waned? Or something else.'

'Something else,' Evie managed.

'Right?' Both a statement and an encouragement to continue.

Evie chose to ignore the latter. She couldn't bring herself to tell anyone, least of all in front of Max, that it was because her attraction wasn't reciprocated.

So she flailed around in her head for an alternative explanation that might sound convincing, but nothing came.

'Evie…?' Arabella urged gently, smiling kindly as Evie could only stare helplessly at her.

Evie opened her mouth but nothing came out.

'Let me get another of these for you.' The surgeon stood up unexpectedly. 'I'll be back in a moment.'

Evie watched her leave gratefully. Clearly Arabella Goodwin was not only a good surgeon but a compassionate individual. This was a perfect excuse to give Evie and Max a moment together, and Evie a chance to compose herself. The woman couldn't have known that Evie could easily have clung onto the woman's immaculately tailored suit and begged her not to leave herself and Max alone in the room.

As the door closed with a soft click Evie stared into her lap, waiting for the inevitable questions.

'You're still…attracted to me?'

He actually sounded surprised, and a little put out, and for a moment Evie forgot her embarrassment. She jerked her head up to stare at him. *The man did look in the mirror, didn't he?*

'Yes,' she answered slowly. 'I can't help that you don't feel the same. My kidney…situation is hardly a turn-on, but you don't have to act as though I'm so completely undesirable as a woman. You were attracted to me, too, once.'

'Is that what you think?'

'That you were attracted to me?' Evie was confused.

'No—' he actually clicked his tongue at her '—that I don't find you desirable.'

She barked out a humourless laugh.

'I think the fact you walked out on me the other day, whilst I was lying practically naked on the bed, is pretty much all the evidence I need.'

'Because I thought I was taking advantage of you,' he exclaimed in a low voice. 'You're only a week post-op. A *major* op, I should add, and you needed my help to even wash your hair in the shower. And there I was, reacting to you. I thought you felt somehow…obligated to me.'

Obligated? Evie's head raced. *No wonder he'd looked so disgusted. But not at her, as she'd assumed. At himself.*

A bubble of happiness wound its way up inside her chest.

'So you don't find me undesirable? Unattractive?'

'I think our curtailed week last year makes it clear just how desirable I find you,' he refuted, his voice thicker than usual.

But any response died on her tongue as the door opened up again and the surgeon walked back in.

So, Max had *wanted her?*

Had he really walked out because he was disgusted at himself, wanting her the way she'd wanted him? Had he really stayed away because he hadn't been sure he could control himself around her and not, as she had surmised, because he had abandoned her?

She chanced another look at Max, who was now also toying with the pamphlet the nephrologist had placed on the table.

A grin played at the corners of her mouth.

She wondered if it was time for a bit of fun. Everything had been so serious lately. Fears weighing so heavily on her, between her own health and Imogen's. And the shock of finding out he had a daughter must have been incredible for Max. But what if they could rediscover some of the fun they'd once shared? The wild side they'd seen in each other during their brief fling.

Yes, the sex had been incredible. But they'd also had fun, laughing and joking in such a way that any outsider would have thought they were in a relationship rather than just indulging in a brief fling before Max disappeared overseas.

Was it possible? Or was it a foolhardy idea? There was only one way to find out.

It was like a switch clicking in Evie's brain as a cheeky thought slid inside.

'I didn't lose interest in sexual intimacy.' She met her nephrologist's eye boldly. She couldn't risk looking to her side. 'I still thought about it, even if I didn't have the opportunity I'd had before my daughter was born. I thought about it a lot, in fact. Especially in the beginning, and then again in the last week before my operation.'

When she'd moved in with Max. Let him work that one out. In her peripheral vision, she could see his head twisting around to look at her, but she didn't dare acknowledge him for fear of laughing.

'That's interesting,' her surgeon noted, oblivious to the significance of the statement. 'And did you feel able to act on it?'

'Not really,' she answered honestly. 'Having an infant isn't exactly conducive. And then there was the dialysis as we talked about before. Although they weren't the only factors.'

'And how do you feel now?'

'Now?' She affected an air of nonchalance. 'I feel very much back to my old self already.'

'So where does that leave us?' Max's deep voice reverberated around the room.

Evie twisted her head around. A wry smile hovered on his lips as his eyes narrowed at her. He'd clearly decided two could play at that game. She felt a kick of pleasure low in her abdomen, rippling down through her core.

'Let me be clearer,' he added robustly. 'Is Evie ready for us to be intimate again? Is that normal?'

'Well, for the most part, I'd say that's entirely up to Evie.' Arabella smiled. 'And I hesitate to use words like *normal*, Max. You know as well as anyone how differently patients can bounce back after any operation.'

Evie could practically feel the anticipation warming her skin. It felt good. She felt alive in a way she hadn't in a very long time.

'But in your case,' the surgeon addressed Evie again, 'where you had a willing donor and therefore didn't have to wait for your transplant or spend too long on dialysis, it's a very positive sign.'

'I see,' Max growled.

'So, Evie, you'll probably find you feel ready for sexual intimacy sooner rather than later. And I really would encourage you, if you do feel well and *want* to resume intimacy, to start exploring it together as a couple.'

'Together,' Evie echoed confidently. 'Got it.'

'However, we do advise you to avoid penetrative intercourse for four to six weeks after your transplant. This is purely to allow the incision site time to heal and not to do with causing any kind of damage to the transplant itself, you understand.'

Oh, no, that had to be a cruel joke, right?

'Don't let that put you off exploring your changing libido as a couple, however. Many people get confused and think that sex only refers to the actual penetrative act of intercourse. However, love-making can include multiple things.'

'Such as hugging? Kissing? Touching each other?' Evie asked, beginning to enjoy herself.

'Exactly.'

Evie might have known not to underestimate Max.

'And what about more than that?' His low voice rumbled through her chest, winding a hot path down. Lower and lower. Images of his tongue skilfully caressing her until he brought her to orgasm filled her head, and a shaft of heat shot through her.

'Again, that's entirely up to you. As long as it isn't too vigorous and therefore doesn't put too much strain on the incision whilst it's knitting.' Professor Goodwin leafed through her notes. 'And once the four to six weeks are up, be aware that fertility in a woman, post-transplant, can increase and, whilst oral contraception can be taken, we would recommend using the barrier method.'

Not as sexy but a valid point, Evie conceded.

'Some institutions recommend you don't become pregnant for at least a year after your transplant, even with stable kidney function, whilst others say two years. Here, we prefer to say eighteen months to two years.'

'That won't be a problem,' Max announced confidently, leaving Evie to wonder whether that was because he had every intention of using protection this time. Or no intention of needing anything to start with.

'Okay.' The nephrologist nodded. 'Then let's move on to your serum creatinine levels and how we expect these check-ups to progress during the next few weeks.'

CHAPTER TEN

MAX LEFT EVIE to complete the final tests whilst he checked on the recovery of the patients.

It was a welcome escape. The air had been loaded with expectation since their conversation with Arabella Goodwin. They were both acutely aware that once they left the hospital to go back home, sex would be on both their minds. And, despite everything that had been said, Max was still conscious of not wanting to push Evie into anything she wasn't ready for.

He saw the person lingering outside his office long before the woman saw him. Something about the way she was hovering intrigued him, shifting from one foot to the other, playing with her long hair and toying with her clothing, first pushing the sleeves of her flannel shirt up in the heat of the hospital, then pulling them down again. He crossed the heavy-duty linoleum hallway in a couple of long strides.

'Do you need something?'

She jumped back from the doorway to glance nervously at him. She could be here to see anyone, but instinct told him she was one of Evie's troubled teens.

'I was wondering about Dr Parker? I didn't realise her transplant was last week and she'd already been discharged. They told me to come and see you.'

'Right.' He wasn't prepared to give anything away.

'How...how did the doc's transplant go?' the young woman asked tentatively.

His eyes swept over her. The flannel shirt—incongruously heavy for the day's temperatures—was open over a lightweight top and trousers, but it was as the young woman messed with her sleeves again that Max caught sight of the scars that lay on her forearms. Multiple thin, parallel lines of silvery-white scars from razor blade or knife lacerations.

Hastily the young woman pulled the sleeves down again, her eyes sliding away from his for a moment, before changing her mind, standing a little taller and making herself meet his glare.

The tacit action garnered his respect, but still he was guarded.

'The transplant went very smoothly,' he answered finally. 'Dr Parker responded very well to the procedure.'

The young woman's relief was visible.

'Good. That's good. Great, in fact. Where is she staying? Can we come and see her?'

'She needs her rest,' Max cut in pointedly. Evie hadn't once mentioned expecting a visit from an ex-patient to him.

'I know she's still recovering,' the woman agreed. 'I just wanted to know she was all right. They won't tell me anything, even though Dr Parker said she'd put my name down to visit as soon as she was cleared for visitors.'

'She doesn't need her focus to be split right now. Do you understand?'

The young woman's brow furrowed in confusion. He suppressed a stab of frustration and smoothed his voice out.

'Dr Parker is very committed to her work, I appreciate that, even though she hasn't practised for quite a few months now, but she needs to take the time to recover and look after herself. If she feels she's needed somewhere else then she's going to try to rush the healing process in order to get back to work.'

He was surprised to see the woman offer a soft smile of recognition.

'Yes. I can just see her doing that. Well, can you tell her that I was here because I wanted to know she was okay? We all did.'

'All?' It was Max's turn to frown.

She jerked her head towards the waiting room chairs down the hall where a group of kids, surrounded by a cluster of small bunches of flowers, home-made fruit baskets and cards waited. They were all watching the exchange between Max and the woman intently, without crowding the two of them, which was why he hadn't noticed them before.

'Who are they?'

'Some of the kids from the centre.'

A lot of the kids from the centre by the look of it. And gifts from even more of them, judging by the mini-mountain. Max stared in shock.

'You look surprised, but Dr Parker has helped so many of us turn our lives around. That's a big deal.'

She narrowed her eyes, assessing him, then clearly decided she had nothing to lose.

'You saw my scars.' She lifted her still-covered arms before dropping them back down to her sides. Nevertheless she met his stare head-on, her chin tilting defiantly.

'I used to self-harm for years, ever since I was

a kid. I couldn't even admit it to myself, let alone tell my family. Eight years ago I met Dr Parker and I've been cut-free for seven years now, and I'm working on keeping it that way.'

'Understood,' Max acknowledged.

Max considered the strong young woman standing in front of him, surprised at her inner strength and matter-of-fact way of talking to him.

'So you're all here just to see how Evie...Dr Parker is?' He eyed the group with fresh eyes.

'Yes. Dr Parker was there for us, supporting us, when we needed her. Now we all have good futures and she was hugely responsible for that. So we just felt this was *our* chance to be here for *her*, now.'

Evie clearly meant a lot to them, and he knew the feeling was mutual. Having to resign her post must have been an agonising decision for Evie to have made.

'So, will you give the gifts to Dr Parker, and tell her we were here?'

The woman's voice broke into his musings.

'Of course.' He dragged himself back to the present but his words were sincere.

'Okay.'

'Okay,' he echoed thoughtfully, watching as the group gathered themselves together, offering him a selection of nods, smiles and even a tentative farewell wave or two.

These kids to whom Evie meant so much.

Gathering up as many of the cards and gifts as he could, he began the first of several trips to his office. He'd load them into the car later. At least it might give them a distraction. Something else to talk about other than the inevitable after today.

It was only as he entered with the final armful that he heard Evie's voice behind him, in the corridor.

'Max?' Her hazy tone filled him with emotions he didn't recognise. 'What are all those?'

'Gifts for you. They were dropped off today,' he answered honestly. 'I'll bring them home at some point and you can look at them when you've rested. Today's check-up must have taken it out of you.'

'Yeah, I'm pretty beat,' she agreed sheepishly.

'Then I guess it's a good job I anticipated this and brought you special fuel to keep you going until we get home and eat.'

With a flourish, he produced a muffin from his pocket, unsure whether she would remember.

'White chocolate and raspberry. You remembered?'

He had expected confusion at worst, a laugh of recognition at best, but he hadn't been prepared for the intense look she suddenly shot him. A look that told him she'd already fast-forwarded past their impulsive encounter that very first evening and to the five nights that had followed. And the flush that leapt to her cheeks, the way her eyes rapidly dilated, convinced him that X-rated images were flicking through her head. The same X-rated images that were now flashing through his brain.

His body tightened in primal response.

He coughed, trying to clear his head. The white-chocolate muffin was supposed to have made her chuckle. A thoughtful gesture. Yet now he couldn't seem to shake this electric charge from coursing around his whole being.

'I'll go and get Imogen from the crèche.' He didn't want her wandering through the main hospital exposing herself to any number of germs or viruses. 'Take the car keys. I'll meet you in the car.'

The conversation with the surgeon had brought up the physical side of their relationship again, and it didn't look as though either of them were going to be able to contain it, now it was out there.

The sooner they gave into it, the better.

'Is everything okay, Max?'

Since she'd discovered Max really did still want

her the way she wanted him, she'd been unsuccessfully striving to ignore the way the atmosphere felt
as though it were *fizzing* around them. Their conversation had been stilted on the drive home, even
though they'd both been trying. Perhaps too hard.

Whilst Imogen had been awake they'd had common ground to talk, but now she'd gone to sleep,
with just the two of them, it was back to strained
politeness. Not what she'd expected after the fun
of their exchange in the nephrologist's office. It
felt as if they were taking two steps back for every
step forward.

'Those gifts you saw me with earlier, they were
from a group of your former patients, your so-
called troubled teens,' he announced suddenly.

The conversation starter took her by surprise.

'Really?'

'Well, I say teens, but one of them looked more
like she was in her twenties. Long dark hair, self-
harm scars on her inside forearms?'

'Sally came to hospital?' Evie fought to keep her
tone light. 'With which others? Why didn't you tell
them to wait?'

'Sally,' he mused. 'I didn't know. I never asked
her name. And I certainly wasn't going to suggest they wait for you—you're still too vulnerable
for that many visitors. Remember—no confined

spaces, no peak-hour transport, no big welcome-home party.'

'I know. How *was* Sally, then?' Evie changed the subject. 'Still doing well?'

'Yes, according to her.' He drew his lips into a thin line. 'But she's no longer one of your patients. Not since you gave up your position and moved away.'

'She's a friend.'

He clicked his tongue.

'You need to learn the difference between a patient and a friend.'

'And you need to learn not to be so dispassionate about either.'

She tensed, preparing for an argument. None came.

'I was thinking something not too dissimilar.'

'You were?' That didn't sound like Max.

'As it happens,' he confirmed tightly, but didn't elaborate. 'So, Sally said she'd been with you for eight years.'

'No, I've known her for eight years but she hasn't been my patient for the last five of them.'

'So she never talks about any problems.'

'I told you, she's a friend. Friends do discuss problems sometimes, you know. But I don't talk to her in exactly the same way I did when it was purely doctor-patient.'

'What kind of problems?'

He sounded genuinely interested, rather than interrogating her. But still, she didn't want to break any confidences.

'I don't feel it's my place to discuss things she's told me in confidence.'

'I thought you said it wasn't a doctor-patient relationship any more.'

'It isn't. Not telling you is a matter of choice, not ethical boundaries.'

'I see. It was only that she seemed very open when I talked to her.'

That was true. Sally was open.

'I suppose you're right. Sally's always felt that by talking about what she's been through it will bring it to more people's attention and lessen the stigma of it—especially considering she's managed to turn her life around, get a good degree and good life experience. But she still can't seem to get a job, because every time anyone sees those scars they discount her without another thought.'

'That really bothers you, doesn't it?' He was suddenly curious.

'Yes, it does. Because she fought hard to understand why it started, what her triggers are, and what alternative outlets worked for her so she didn't harm herself any more. But because the visual scars are always there, she's never allowed to move forward and get on with her life.'

'Okay, so tell me how she started.'

She hesitated again, about to tell him again that it wasn't her place to tell him. But that wasn't what Sally would want.

Evie gave an almost imperceptible shrug.

'She started self-harming just before she hit her teens. Her parents were going through a particularly acrimonious divorce, which included fighting over custody of her older sister—the more accomplished of the two of them. She felt as though she was the one neither of them wanted.'

'So, why cut? Divorce happens to a lot of kids.'

'And self-harm happens more than you'd think, too. A&E records suggest around fourteen per cent of kids aged between eleven and sixteen can self-harm. But the real figures are likely to be significantly higher because many cases go unreported.'

'How? How does it get missed, Evie?'

His cool, unemotional tone suddenly grated on her. She'd fought daily to convince enough individuals and institutions without having to convince Max as well.

'I don't know. Perhaps because not everyone has people interested enough to notice,' Evie cried in exasperation. 'Or because not everyone is as thick-skinned and self-possessed as the great Maximilian Van Berg. Unlike you, the rest of us are human, and what other people say or how they treat us can hurt.'

'What the hell is that supposed to mean?' he growled angrily.

'It means I hate that these kids sometimes feel they have no one on their side. Some might grow out of it before it gets noticed, especially with boys who find other ways than cutting, which they think is more a girl's thing. But just because they punch themselves, or walls, or initiate fights where they know they'll get hurt doesn't make it any less self-harming than cutting is.'

'You're saying if boys fight they're replacing cutting themselves with getting beaten up?' he said scornfully. 'Boys fight, it's a normal part of growing up. It's a way of letting off a bit of steam against another kid who has got under your skin. Better than the social exclusion some girls use against others. Isn't it that kind of ostracising which contributes to some kids self-harming?'

'Yes, but I'm not talking about evenly matched boys taking the occasional argument into the playground, Max, I'm talking about some boys who purposefully get into fights every single day, especially if they choose older or bigger kids who they know will easily beat them up and hurt them.'

'A broken nose, even a broken rib, depending on who they choose to fight?' Max demanded unexpectedly 'If kids call them names because they have a big nose, or ears which stick out?'

'Sometimes it's that,' Evie agreed. 'Other times it's following a traumatic event. But it doesn't even have to be so clear-cut. It might just be a sense of feeling they don't measure up somehow. And they might not fight other kids, they might wait until no one's around and punch walls, or deliberately put themselves into dangerous situations. That's when it goes from boys fighting as a normal part of growing up, to them finding a way of self-harming without actually cutting.'

She expected him to come back at her. Instead he stared at her, unexpectedly silent, his face set into an expression she'd never seen before. It worried her.

'What is it?'

'Nothing, I'm sorry.' He seemed instantly contrite.

'Max?'

'It's nothing.' He was really making an effort to sound nonchalant. Anyone else might have bought it. But not her.

'Max? What's wrong? Talk to me.'

CHAPTER ELEVEN

MAX FROZE. HER WORDS were like an unexpected bombshell. And then it was as if a red-hot rod seared through his gut.

Evie had no idea of the emotional Pandora's box her words had just opened. How could she? He'd never told her. He'd never even realised it himself. He'd seen it in people like Dean, although he hadn't recognised it for what it was. But himself? Never.

And yet, for the first time in his life, he felt as though he was looking at someone he could actually trust.

It wasn't just about the sex.

The thought slammed into him like a lorry jackknifing into his chest. For all the banter and teasing in Arabella's office, he knew Evie was more than just that one fling. And it wasn't just about the daughter who would now connect them for ever. He *wanted* that connection with Evie. He *wanted* her to be in his life. Her and Imogen.

And that meant talking to her, confiding in her, in a way he'd never anticipated confiding in anyone in his life. It meant trusting Evie. But he could do it, because he owed it to her to be as honest with her as she'd now been with him.

'Was that you, Max? Were you that kid?' she asked gently, and he was reminded that he wasn't just trusting Evie, the mother of his child. He was trusting Dr Parker. He didn't know who he was talking to right now, but he didn't suppose it mattered, just as long as he talked.

'I used to come home every night with a bloody nose, a black eye or cracked ribs,' he started hesitantly.

'Why?'

He shrugged, unable to find the words. He'd shut off his past so firmly that he'd almost forgotten about the fighting. Now it was hard to articulate it.

'Did you want the attention from your parents?'

'No,' he snorted. 'And if I had it would have had the opposite effect. They found it hard enough to tell me they were proud of me when I achieved all they expected of me—they could never have dealt with talking about any problems I was having. I think that would have made them retreat into their careers even more.'

'Your parents didn't think you *ever* had problems? Almost every kid has a problem growing up one way or another.'

'Not me,' Max disagreed. 'As far as they were concerned, I was intelligent with a stable background and parents who made sure I went to school, and did my homework to get good grades.'

'What about talking about general growing-up issues?'

'What issues?' he asked flatly, echoing his parents' attitude. 'I was a kid—how could I possibly have issues?'

'So you started fighting?'

'Yeah. I didn't like bullies, so it started there. If I saw another kid getting picked on I'd go after the bully. They got bigger and harder, and I got angrier.'

'How long did it go on for?'

'A while.'

Longer than he cared to admit.

'And what did your parents do?'

'Nothing.' He closed his eyes for a moment. 'One single teacher noticed and took me under his wing. He got me into a mandatory after-school sports programme with swimming, cycling and running.'

'And the fighting stopped?'

'Yeah. All the kids had gone home by the time I got out, so the same opportunities to fight were gone. Besides, I'd always been too busy and too knackered to fight after that.'

'And your parents?'

'It was like it never happened.'

'You're in contact with them?'

There was an odd note in her voice.

'They called when I got back from Gaza.'

'To tell you they were proud of you?' she guessed.

'No,' he answered flatly. 'They called to say they were glad I was safe and to remind me I should write a medical paper on the medical practices out there.'

'Do you...that is...what do you think they'd make of Imogen?'

'Honestly? I don't know.'

They would probably tell him that he'd made a grave mistake, and that he'd never be able to focus on his career the same way with some kid in the background. But he couldn't tell Evie that. He couldn't hurt her that way.

It shocked Max to realise that he might have felt a similar way himself once, before Imogen had burst into his life and enriched it in a way he would never have considered possible.

She shook her head but her silence spoke volumes, her eyes trained on the coffee mug, around which her hands were cupped tightly.

'Just don't be so quick to believe nothing has ever got to me,' he continued, his smile not quite reaching his eyes. 'I'm not as infallible as you seem to think.'

Or indeed as he had thought himself. Shocked by his own revelations, Max changed the conversation to something less charged. Something that he knew Evie would jump to discuss.

'Tell me more about Sally.'

Her questioning glance made him smile.

'I'm interested. Please, humour me.'

'Okay,' she said slowly. 'Like I said, she struggled with issues of feeling unwanted. Like...you, I guess. She somehow managed to get herself into university but she wasn't ready for the demands of the course and she really started to spiral. She started going out clubbing and drinking, every night to excess.'

'Like most students.'

'Not exactly. Then she started on recreational drugs. But when she was with the campus counsellor about to be thrown off her course she had enough guts to tell her what was going on. That's when she came to me.'

'And you helped her to turn it all around?' Max asked.

'Yes, but only because she wanted to do it herself. She just needed the support. There's obviously a lot more to it than that, but ultimately she managed to get back into uni and graduate well. She could get a good job, too, if only health-assessment boards would look beyond the scars of her past to see what she's like now.'

'I could do something with them.'

'Sorry?'

'I could help her with the scars,' he repeated quietly.

'How? There are too many of them over too large an area, and they're deep into the subcutaneous level. How would you eradicate them?'

'I'm not saying I can eradicate them,' Max replied. 'But I could abrade the cicatrised area and then use a split thickness skin graft to over-graft. She'll still have a scar, but it won't look like those lined scars from cutting any more.'

'So people won't stigmatise her?' Evie's voice

caught. 'That would be incredible, but she can't afford it.'

'I know that.' He blew out a breath. 'Call it my charitable act.'

'You would do that for her?'

'I'd do that for you,' he responded quietly. And part of him felt the need to do it for himself, as well. It was incredible but after his unexpected confession he wasn't dwelling on the past; in truth he felt lighter than he had ever felt before. Telling his secrets to Evie had been cathartic, not because it was her job but because he felt as though he was sharing a part of himself with Evie that no one else even knew existed. Right at this moment, Max knew he'd never felt as close a connection to another human being as he felt to Evie.

But he knew his confession had startled her, even though she was doing her best to conceal it. So right now he needed them to get back to the fun of earlier that day, and forget everything else but the fact that they'd both realised how much they still wanted each other.

'Oh, and one last thing.' He shot her a wicked smile. 'So there are no further misunderstandings, let me make it perfectly clear. I still want you. Whenever you're ready. You're sexy, exceptionally desirable and, for what it's worth, you're also someone I want to be with.'

And Evie could take from that whatever she wanted.

'Our daughter's out for the count and she looks perfectly angelic.' Evie managed a shaky smile a few hours later as she descended the stairs from checking on the baby. 'You want to see her?'

She was stalling; she couldn't help it. The need for Max, intimately and completely, had been gnawing at her ever since their easy exchange in the nephrologist's office. She'd spent so long feeling bad about herself since her illness, but Max was the one person who made her feel like a whole woman again.

The whole day had been one of revelations. The fact that he hadn't abandoned her the other night but that he'd been uncertain as to how much she wanted him, had always wanted him. His acceptance that her job meant so much to her, and his offer of helping Sally. But, most incredibly, Max's confession about his childhood, which had made her feel simultaneously closer to him, yet all the more disconnected.

She needed to tell him. But the closer she got to him, the more scared she was of him turning against her. So she would first need to convince him that they could be more, so much more, than just co-parents of a beautiful daughter. They could be a proper family.

And even though she wanted to prove to Max that the two of them could be so much more than just incredible sex, right now it still seemed like the best place to start.

So, when he took her hand and drew her up the hallway, Evie silenced the last voice of doubt.

'Tonight I'll take your word for how angelic our daughter is. But right now, Evangeline,' he uttered, his voice gravelly with desire, 'I don't want to wait any longer for you.'

In spite of her fears Evie actually giggled as she raced him up the hall, tumbling to her bedroom together and stopping still by the door.

She could feel Max's breath on her skin. Her heart picked up speed as her own breathing came shallow and fast and when she dared a glance at Max, he was watching the rapid rise and fall of her chest. Then his mouth crashed onto hers with exquisite need.

She responded without hesitation, drinking in his taste, his touch. He dipped his head to kiss a scorching trail from her lips, down her throat and to the sensitive hollow. Arching towards him as he dropped his hand to lazily skim the exposed skin of her chest then cup her breast, his thumb drawing slow whorls over her hard nipple through her top, the fabric proving a frustrating barrier for her. But Max didn't seem to be in any great hurry. He seemed happy teasing her, exploring, nibbling.

She slid her fingers up his thigh, making for his crotch, a thrill coursing through her as she felt him hard beneath the rough material, but his other hand reached down to still any further movements.

'Slow down, Evie.'

His voice was thick with longing and he practically growled, but it only turned her on even more. She pushed his hand off hers and propelled them both towards the bed, pushing him gently down and moving across him so that she was sitting on his lap, her legs wrapped around him, ignoring the stab of pain at her incision site. She was determined not to wince; she didn't want to give Max any reason to insist they take things slowly.

She shifted, wondering if he could feel the heat from her body, when he sucked in a sharp breath, and she gave a wicked gurgle of triumph. *That would be a* yes, *then.*

Evie slid her hands down and tugged at the hem of his tee shirt, pulling it up and only pausing in their kissing for long enough to haul it over his head. She balled the fabric and threw it across the room with a grin.

'Making a point?' he muttered, amused.

'Might be.'

Her hands reacquainted themselves with the muscled chest she'd been dreaming about for the last twelve months. Weaving her fingers into the smattering of dark hair, Evie pushed him back onto the bed, her eyes grazing over him hungrily.

'Like what you see?'

It was a challenge. Almost a dare. Evie smirked at him wickedly, feeling more sexually assured than she ever had before.

'Purely a professional assessment.'

Max quirked one eyebrow.

'Oh, really, *Dr Parker*?'

'Mmm-hmm,' she murmured, tracing an un-hurried line along the tense chest muscles, which were, incredibly, even more impressive than she'd recalled. Lowering her head, Evie pressed a kiss into each of them. 'Pectorals.'

'You liked your anatomy classes?' he managed.

'I did.' She dipped her head lower. 'Rectus ab-dominis. Upper.'

'Yup,' but his voice quivered slightly as she kissed again.

Evie moved across.

'Transversus abdominis.'

Another kiss. And this time he didn't offer any kind of quip.

Lower again, Evie ignored the pain shooting across her side. She wanted him more than she was prepared to give in to anything else. Which meant she was ready.

'Evie...?'

'Shh...' she instructed. 'I'm fine, don't ruin it.'

The moment with Max felt too precious, and too fragile to risk breaking. Besides, she needed to prove this to herself. She wasn't just mentally recovered, she was almost physically healed, too.

'Oblique.'

The requisite kiss and she could feel his body straining against her forearm. A sense of power surged through her. He was relinquishing control to her because she was claiming it. It was a heady feeling. She moved back to his middle.

'Which brings us back to rectus abdominis. Lower.' Her voice sounded thick with lust as she dropped a final kiss before straightening up to offer him an innocent stare. 'So, *Mr* Van Berg, where should I go from here?'

Her hands moved to his belt buckle but before she could do anything else Max pulled her to him, hooking his hands around her backside, and stood up with her legs still wrapped around his hips.

'You made your point,' he growled. 'You're healing well. But I can make a point, too.'

Before she could worry that he was going to back away from her like last time, Max set her back on the bed and reached for her zip, waiting a few tantalising moments before he divested her of her top. Her bra didn't last much longer. Then he pressed her gently down until her back sank into the soft mattress, and covered her body with his, taking care not to place any weight on her. Skin to skin now, the muscles Evie had just been kissing grazed her breasts, making her nipples stiffen even more in response.

Obligingly, Max lowered his head and circled them with a hot, wet tongue before taking them into his mouth. She squirmed underneath him, desperate for more, but he locked her down, taking his delicious time.

It was pointless to resist, Evie reluctantly concluded a few moments later as she gave herself up to the butterflies currently performing spinning and twirling Viennese waltzes throughout her entire core. When he seared her skin with his lips it was all she could do to hold still, contenting herself with familiarising her hands with the solid contours of his back and shoulders. And when he raised his head back up to reclaim her mouth she matched him, demanding kiss for demanding kiss. Evie ached to hold him in her hand again, feel him rock solid and so turned on by her that she could barely circle him with her fingers. But he held himself too far away, making *her* the sole focus of the evening's intimacy, and, given the skill with which Max was arousing her, it wasn't exactly a hardship to relinquish the power again. By the time he finally trailed a line with his tongue down her lower abdomen and to the waistband of her jersey trousers, she was powerless to contain her moan of anticipation.

The last of the Steri-strips had come off and the scar was looking less angry and welt-like than it had a few days ago, so Evie forced herself not to cover up the incision as Max paused for a moment to inspect it. Satisfied, he finally slid her jersey trousers down over her hips, cocking an eyebrow at her as he saw she'd replaced her comfy knickers with a scrap of lace that sat well below the scar.

It was on the tip of her tongue to claim that was all she had left, having thrown the rest of her underwear in the wash, but she figured that might be as transparent as the turquoise lace, and instead she ignored the unspoken question, focusing instead on the aching need for him to touch her right where she needed him most.

As if reading her thoughts, Max hooked his finger around the scrap and brushed a knuckle against the aching bud. Evie gasped, instinctively lifting her hips to deepen the contact but he moved his hand away again, in exquisite torment. She laced her fingers through his hair.

'Max.' The raw voice didn't sound like her own. 'I need you inside me.'

He barely paused in his attentions.

'Not tonight.'

It was a wrench but Evie forced herself to pull away from him, lifting her shoulders off the bed so that she could see him.

'You heard the nephrologist—four to six weeks post-op,' he reminded her, moving to lower his head again, but Evie pressed her hand against him, stopping him.

How could he sound so casual about it? This was torturous for her.

'Max...'

'That's a minimum of two weeks, three days and twenty-two and a half hours.'

'You're counting in days and hours?' A gurgle of laughter escaped her. He wasn't as composed about all this as she'd thought. And she was glad about that.

'From the moment we made that damned deal,' Max ground out. 'And it's taking more willpower than you can possibly imagine not to take you right now. So will you please shut up, and let me concentrate on just...*exploring* you?'

Evie hesitated. This wasn't exactly going as she'd planned in her head.

'Max...' Her objection evaporated from her brain as Max pulled aside the lace material again and flicked his tongue against her swollen skin. Unable to keep herself upright any longer, she fell back onto the pillows as he sucked and licked at the sensitive bud, sending mini fireworks exploding through her belly.

Max slid his finger inside her, his mouth unrelenting in its devilish benevolence as she jiggled in response. She gave a guttural moan moments before the orgasm shattered through her, and Max instinctively slid his hands around to hold her bottom in place, stopping her from writhing away; his tongue and finger coaxing a longer, more intense orgasm than she'd ever known. Evie's body shook with the impact of it as she cried out his name, but he didn't let her go until he was convinced he couldn't tease anything more out of her.

Falling back down, she held her breath in anticipation until Max pulled himself up the bed to haul her into his arms. Evie nestled against his shoulder gratefully, wishing she would never have to leave the security of his embrace. It had been too long. Not just since the last time she'd had sex. But since the last time she'd been with Max. There would never be anyone else for her who would match up to him.

But if there was to be any chance that this could be more than *just sex*, she knew she was going to have to start by telling him about the fact she'd met his parents. And she needed to do it now.

Okay, tomorrow.

Or maybe the day after that.

She needed to be more sure of how Max felt about her. His love for his daughter was clear, but what then?

Lying down, Evie allowed Max to snuggle her in his arms. For all her efforts to take the lead, in the end her confidence hadn't been as high as she'd hoped and she'd been only too happy to let Max take over. So for now she was just going to enjoy this moment. She'd been dreaming of it for long enough.

CHAPTER TWELVE

'SO THIS IS Silvertrees Old Town?' Evie breathed. 'It's incredible up here, so peaceful. And I can see for miles.'

Max watched her angle her head to let the rays of sun heat her skin, despite the cool breeze of the high viewing platform, her hands resting on hip-height grey stone wall.

'It *is* stunning,' he agreed quietly.

'Do you get chance to come here that much?'

He dropped his hand to cradle the back of Imogen's head as she nestled against his chest in her baby harness, buying himself a moment to think whether he wanted to answer.

Somehow, it felt like something particularly personal. Ever since they'd first been intimate again, he'd begun to open up more and more to Evie, trusting her in a way he had never trusted anyone before.

'When I can, usually on a run,' he found himself admitting with more ease than he'd anticipated.

'Especially if I want to clear my head before a particularly complex operation. Although I come here less during tourist season—you wouldn't believe how busy it gets then.'

'Really?' She glanced around, taking in the boarded-up stalls. Barely a soul was around at this moment, except for a few artists sketching or painting the spectacular vista. Only the ticket office was open, although a couple of owners were taking advantage of the off-season to repair and repaint their little shops built into the rock face.

Max nodded, feeling himself relax more and more as Evie seemed to fall for the beauty of the place the same way he once had. It was like another small confirmation of how well matched they were.

'It used to be Silvertrees itself before the hospital was built a mile out of town and all the housing sprung up around *that*. Then the hospital took the name Silvertrees and this place became the Old Town, or Outer Silvertrees,' he explained. 'How is it you've never been here?'

With a rueful smile, Evie lifted her shoulders at his light teasing.

'I only ever came here to go to the hospital, either for work or for myself. I didn't even know they had a funicular railway here.'

He arched his eyes in surprise.

'Did you know it was built in the late nineteenth century?'

'Oh, right.' She only hesitated a fraction of a moment before following suit. 'But it's electricity-powered?'

'Good eye.' He nodded, impressed. 'It was rebuilt in the forties specifically for that reason. And the original wooden cars were replaced with lightweight aluminium carriages. But the original line used a simple system of gravity and water. They pumped water into a two-thousand-gallon tank underneath the top car until it outweighed the lower car. Once the top car reached the bottom station they emptied the tank and pumped it back up to a tank at the top station.'

'You know a lot about it,' Evie remarked with a grin.

'I originally wanted to be an engineer when I was growing up,' he answered evenly. No need for Evie to know that she was the only person, outside his parents, who he'd ever told.

Still she glanced at him sharply.

'What happened?'

Max opened his mouth; best to tell her that he'd changed his mind as he'd grown up.

'My parents told me not to be so stupid. That I

was going to become a surgeon like them, and that was all there was to it.'

He forced a smile as her eyes slid over him, assessing.

'Oh. Well, for what it's worth, there are thousands and thousands of patients out there who are very glad you were their surgeon.'

'Thanks.' He grinned wryly. 'I appreciate you not trying to psychoanalyse me.'

'At least out loud,' she couldn't resist. 'For the record, though, I can also see you taking that funicular-style technology with you to some foreign country. And manually building one out there for them, if they needed it.'

'Yeah, I guess that's the geeky side of me coming out.'

'I like it,' Evie offered shyly before teasing him. 'It's better than being the *demon of discipline*.'

'Oh, I see. Hitting below the belt, are we?' he quipped as he stepped towards her, careful not to crush Imogen as he drew Evie into his arms.

The kiss was slow and thorough, and full of promise.

Something was changing deep inside him, something fundamental. It felt as though Evie was finally unlocking a part of himself he'd never even known existed, and he liked it.

More than liked it. He welcomed it.

Eventually they pulled apart with reluctance as Imogen made her objections known. Evie dropped a kiss on her daughter's head before lifting her head to meet his gaze. Something indefinable *clicked* inside him, and Max slid protective arms around both of them.

'I think I could live here.'

'Sorry?' He pulled his head back to look at her.

'In Silvertrees,' Evie clarified nervously. 'Back at my brother's house when you first talked about Imogen and I coming up here, I told you that I wouldn't want to move that far away from him or Annie. But, if it meant you and Imogen having a closer relationship, then I could learn to love living here.'

None of the words that came into his head seemed to adequately express his emotions at Evie's generosity of spirit. Instead, he just pressed a hard kiss to her lips, gratified when she smiled her relieved acceptance.

But that indescribable *something* still hovered on the periphery of his mind. What *was* it? And why was he finding it so difficult to express?

'We'd better get back so you can get ready for your three-week check-up.'

They were starting to extend the time between

check-ups. It was a good sign, it meant Evie was making good progress.

In companionable silence, they wandered off the viewing platform and slowly rambled alongside the long stretch of stone wall towards the railway, which would take them back down towards the lower section of Old Town.

'Mr Van Berg?'

They both whirled around as a man hurried towards them, a large sheet, clearly just torn from his sketchpad, in his outstretched hand. It was one of the artists from before.

'You saved my sister's hand a couple of years ago when she got it crushed in a car door.' His voice was heavy with gratitude. 'We never knew how to repay you but…well, I hope this goes some way towards it.'

Before Max could reply, the man had thrust the painting at him and was hurrying back off up the wide, cobbled tourist route, only turning briefly to wave his hand in acknowledgement. Turning the sketch around, Max lowered his head.

His heart drummed a tom-tom solo in his chest.

'It's amazing,' Evie whispered, her chin resting against his arm.

And it was. A striking likeness of the three of them, capturing the moment Evie had dropped a kiss on their daughter's head, the two of them encircled protectively in his embrace. But more than that, an intense love radiated from the drawing, the lines, fine here and thicker there, drawing the viewer deeper into the picture.

And the simple caption. *Family.*

Max stopped dead. That one word finally gave him a name to that *something* that had *clicked* inside him earlier, to the feeling playing at the edges of his mind.

Family.

The idea of Evie moving to Silvertrees in order that he should enjoy a better relationship with his daughter was commendable, but it wasn't a good enough reason. He needed Evie to want to move here for herself. To be with him. Because he wanted to be with them *both*. He wanted them to be a family in every sense of the word. For ever.

'What is it?' Evie had pivoted in concern as he stopped so abruptly.

'Wait,' he commanded hoarsely, desperately trying to clear his head of the crazy thoughts now swarming.

How much time had he wasted? How much energy? Focussing on his career and excluding the possibility of anything else, anything more, just because he didn't want to be the kind of parent his own had been to him.

Now he knew he never would be like them. It wasn't who he was. He wasn't emotionally unavailable as they were, and Evie had been the one to show him that.

'Max? Is everything all right?'

She was obviously worried, and yet he still didn't know how to tell her. What would he say? It wasn't as if he even knew that she felt the same way he did. What if he told her he wanted more than they'd ever agreed only to scare her off? He suspected she felt as he did, but, then again, family life with him wasn't something she had ever suggested she wanted.

'What about you?' he rasped.

Her eyebrows knitted together in nervous confusion.

'Me?'

'You talked about living here in order that Imogen and I would have a closer relationship. But what about us? Would you and I have a closer relationship, too?'

He heard her breath catch in her throat.

'Is that what you want?'

'It is,' he confirmed without hesitation, but held back from saying anything more.

'Right.' Evie nodded, swallowing hard.

'Is it what you want?' he echoed her question carefully.

She nodded again but said nothing more.

He couldn't be sure what that meant, but in that moment he swore to himself that he'd prove to her they could be, they *should* be, a proper family. In every sense of the word.

Evie quelled the flitting butterflies in her abdomen as she stood in the doorway to Imogen's nursery and watched Max lower their sleeping daughter into the ornate cot. Quietly, she backed away down the hall and into the master bedroom, into which she'd pretty much decamped after that first night of sexual intimacy.

But since their venture into Old Town together five days ago, something had changed. It wasn't just about their sexual intimacy, but about their emotional intimacy.

And that was on a whole new level.

Max loved her. She could feel it. She knew it. And from the moment he'd seen that sketch entitled *Family* she'd known Max knew it, too.

She just didn't know whether he was ready to acknowledge it to her, yet. And so she bit her tongue and reined herself in, wanting him to tell her when he was ready. In his own time.

Which, she had to admit, was having its perks.

Every day that Max tried to tell her he loved her but couldn't, he resorted instead to trying to show her how he felt. Ways which were growing more and more intensely passionate as though to compensate for the words that were eluding him. And Evie had never felt so desired, or needed, or wanton.

But as exquisite as it was, tonight she intended to take matters into her own hands. She'd tried a few nights ago, with her sexual assessment of his anatomy, which had been even more fun than she'd hoped. But in the end, when Max had taken charge again, she'd bottled it and let him. But this time, she was going to run things if only to prove to him that she was the same woman he'd known a year ago, not this vulnerable, ill Evie, as he'd begun to think of her. And if he couldn't tell her he loved her after *that*…well, she was just determined that wouldn't be the case.

She heard Max creeping out of the nursery and heading down the hallway and ducked into the shower room, shedding her clothes quickly and efficiently. It was another boost to her self-esteem that she was now able to do this for herself, a far cry from when she'd needed Max to help her to wash her hair.

This shower experience was going to end up very differently from back then, Evie determined. Just as long as Max adequately interpreted the trail of clothes leading from the bedroom door. Her heart lodged somewhere in her throat; it would be just her luck for the door to have closed on her artfully placed heeled shoe and for Max to walk straight downstairs.

With relief Evie saw his shadow entering the room and heading towards the bathroom door, only hesitating slightly as he heard the sound of running water.

'Everything okay, Evie? Do you need any help?'

She was touched by his consideration. Just because they'd been intimate every night he didn't take it as his right to simply walk in. She licked her lips despite the shower water running over her from head to toe.

'No help.' Good job her voice didn't betray her racing heart. 'But company would be nice.'

Through the steamed glass she watched him round the corner, entering the doorway and approaching the shower. Standing as proudly as she could, she indicated the spacious shower area with a confident jerk of her head.

Her skin heated as his eyes swept slowly over her, taking in the head-to-toe view, darkening appreciatively as the pupils dilated, turning them almost black.

She held out the soaped-up body puff.

'Well, are you going to join me, then?'

He didn't need a third invitation.

Within seconds he'd stripped down and stepped around the expanse of glass. Tall, proud and wickedly masculine, his desire for her was unmistakeable and Evie didn't bother to suppress her grin of delight.

He took the proffered body puff but before he could make use of it, he was pulling her against his hard, already gleaming wet body, and bringing his mouth down on hers. Hot and demanding, more so than any nights before.

She slid her hands around to his back, moving them over strong shoulder muscles, down to his athletic waist, and lower to cup his backside and draw herself closer to him, right against the heat between her legs. Carefully, Evie rocked her hips against him before bringing her hand around to stroke him, gripping him more firmly as he flexed against her. She remembered only too well just how Max had liked it when she'd taken the lead a few times during their fling, and tonight she intended to replicate that. Banish the idea of her as weak and vulnerable, once and for all.

Tightening her grip slightly, she moved harder, faster, all the while nibbling at the hollow of his neck and up to his jawline.

His husky groan sent a shiver rippling down her spine. It felt good to wield sexual power over a man like Max, but she had to be careful; she was barely hanging onto her own sense of control by her fingernails.

She rocked against him again, feeling his whole length flexing, solid against her skin. The sigh escaped her lips before she could stop it, only for Max to react to the sound in the most primitive way. Desire flooded straight down to her core. Parting her legs slightly, she nestled him even deeper against herself, not doubting that he could feel how hot and slick she was. How ready for him.

'Stop,' he managed hoarsely, breaking the contact with what was clearly supreme effort. 'We need to slow it down.'

'No,' whispered Evie cheekily, 'we don't.'

His eyes locked with hers, narrowing slightly as he saw her intent.

'Evie, you've no idea how much I want you, but we can't. Not yet. Your incision—'

'Is fine,' she cut him off before he could finish.

'I checked today. They said it's up to me. It has been almost a month.'

Then she saw it. That brief moment of hesitation before he shook his head.

'No, it's been three weeks, five days. I won't let you risk it. Not yet.'

Too late. She grinned inside. She'd seen all she needed to see. Max wanted her as much as she wanted him, and tonight she didn't intend to wait any longer.

'What difference will two more days make? They're satisfied the wound is healed, that I won't cause any damage or stress on the site. As far as they're concerned, now it's all down to when I feel ready. And I feel ready *now*.' She chuckled weakly, hoping to cover up her nerves.

'That's why you asked me to get Imogen whilst you had that last appointment,' he exclaimed. 'You wanted to ask them without me there.'

'I knew you'd argue we should wait for the full six weeks. But it's my body and I know how strong it is. And I can't wait. I don't want to. I need you and I know you feel the same.' She grinned to soften her next words. 'So will you please just shut up and kiss me, Max?'

She barely had time to exhale after her hurried monologue before his mouth crashed down on hers with a ferocious desire, chasing every other thought from her head. He slid one hand around to slip between her legs. Gripping hold of Max's shoulders, Evie just clung on and prepared to let herself be swept away, but then she recalled the split second before he'd kissed her, and the air was sucked from her chest without warning. The way he'd looked at her—no man had ever looked at her with such intense longing before, making her feel more confident than she ever had.

Summoning all her strength, she pushed him away and took the unused body puff from his hands as she turned the water off. It wasn't exactly what she'd planned but in some ways that made it even better to know that neither of them were completely in control.

'Shall we take this through to the bedroom?' she managed hoarsely before giving an apologetic smile. 'There's protection on the nightstand.'

She might be feeling good enough to bring forward the sex part of things, but she knew there was no point in being stupid and risking a pregnancy on her still-healing body. And by the expression now crossing Max's face that had been one of the worries holding him back.

As if to prove her point, he suddenly bent down and scooped her up into his arms, carrying her out of the shower and through to the bedroom in an echo of that previous encounter. Only this time, Evie was confident it wasn't going to end with him depositing her on the bed and walking out.

She was right. Lowering her down, Max immediately joined her, intent clear in his dark eyes as he began to move down her body trailing whorls on her stomach with his tongue as he moved lower. She fought the urge to simply give herself up to him.

'Uh-uh,' she croaked out, catching his head. 'This time it's my turn. Get on your back.'

Max only paused for a moment before obeying, but when she straddled him and began to move down his body, just as he had with her a moment earlier, he let out a deep groan.

'I don't think I can hold out much longer.' He gritted his teeth. 'You really got me in the shower before, and I've wanted you for too long.'

'I feel the same,' whispered Evie.

She could save that for later; right now she just wanted a release with him. To recapture some of the connection she was sure they'd made a year ago, and to remind them both how it had been before all this transplant business had tarnished things.

Leaning over him to retrieve the condom from

the bedside table, she wasn't prepared when Max reached up and cupped her breasts, his mouth moving from one tight nipple to the other. She shifted to offer him better access, her hands fumbling as she distractedly tried to open the foil packet whilst sensations jolted through her body.

'So beautiful, so perfect,' he murmured against her skin.

But this was about her taking control, she reminded herself through the haze. Pressing her hands to his shoulders to keep him down on the bed, Evie sat up, sliding down his legs enough to access his solid length, putting on a slight show as she languidly sheathed him and revelling in his shallow, faster breathing as his eyes were riveted to her every move.

Everything about Max screamed strength, power, masculinity, but having him lie here now, allowing himself to be at her mercy, gave Evie a sense of control, which she desperately needed. She felt capable, reassured and absolutely all-woman again as she met Max's intense gaze and held it, not allowing herself to look away as she covered him, running her hands over his taut, muscular chest as she slid carefully down to take all of him inside her. As if they were designed to fit together perfectly.

Even as he gasped, his hands gripped her hips to hold her from moving and Evie could feel him holding back, worrying about hurting her. She traced a pattern down his lower abdomen, over his Apollo's belt, and placed her hands over his, lifting them enough to stop him restricting her movements.

'My timings,' she reminded him shakily, before rocking over him and feeling his reaction deep inside her.

'Evie. You're so tight, so wet,' he muttered, finally gripping her hips as if he meant it as he thrust up to meet her movements.

She was too primed, too ready to hold out for long and it seemed that Max hadn't been lying when he'd said the same. Within minutes she felt him stiffen as she exploded, climaxing together as wave after wave crashed over her.

There was no doubt any more that she loved Max, completely and utterly. But if he didn't love her back the same way then she would still always be grateful to him for showing her that, kidney transplant or not, she was still all-woman.

Wanton, desirable, and utterly powerful.

CHAPTER THIRTEEN

'KEEP YOUR EYES closed and walk where I guide you,' instructed Max, careful not to let her bump against Imogen, lodged happily in the baby sling on his chest. It was the first family outing they'd had since that incredible night when they'd slept together again.

'What happened to the brisk training walk you promised me?' She giggled nervously.

'We took a detour first. Keep them closed.'

Trusting Max to lead her safely along, Evie kept her eyes closed but her mind whirred. The last thing she'd seen before Max had asked her to close her eyes was that they'd driven through the stunning National Park and through imposing gates and past a gatehouse lodge onto private parkland. A huge hall had stood in the distance but Max had turned onto a smaller single-track road, past a chapel and a hunting lodge.

That was when he'd first asked her to close her eyes.

The temptation to sneak a peek as the car glided silently along had been almost overwhelming and Evie had drawn on every inch of resolve not to give in to the temptation. Even when the car had finally stopped and parked up, and Max had taken an excruciatingly long time getting Imogen out of her car seat and settled in her sling before he finally came around to lead Evie herself out of the passenger side.

She could feel the heat of the afternoon sunshine on her back, and cobblestones beneath her feet, and was glad of her walking shoes. The air was full of the scent of freshly mown grass, whilst the only sounds were the calls of birds and water, like the rippling of a runnel. And then the clicking of a wooden latch, possibly an outside gate.

Still allowing Max to lead her along, she felt the slight drop in temperature, and just as she was about to assume she'd stepped indoors the heat of the sun hit her again and she realised they'd walked through some kind of archway but were still outside.

She opened her mouth to ask but Max spoke before she could.

'You can open your eyes now.'

Not sure what to expect, Evie obliged. Blinking

in the sunshine, it took her a few moments for her eyes to adjust. She gave a gasp of awe.

She was standing in an expansive cobbled quad, at the centre of which an old stone fountain trickled water into a moss-covered stone animal water trough. Large, multi-leaf sets of sliding doors offered tantalising glimpses of the single-storey rooms inside, a couple of which were already open to reveal a large black baby grand piano.

Turning around, Evie looked up at the double height, yellow sandstone building behind her.

'The old coach house for the main hall,' Max offered by way of explanation. 'Shall we look around?'

'Are we allowed?' she found herself whispering. 'It looks like someone's home now.'

'It is.' Max grinned. 'But it's up for sale.'

It took Evie a few moments to process what he was suggesting.

'You're thinking of moving? To a family house? For you and Imogen?'

Not that it could be considered your average family house. She shook her head in disbelief. *You could house about five families in a place like this.*

'For me and for Imogen. *And* for you,' he corrected, the first hint of nervousness in his voice. 'If that's what you want?'

A family house? For them to be a proper family?

Evie could only gape at him, unable to answer as two warring thoughts crowded out her mind.

It was more than she could have ever dreamed of with Max. But she still hadn't told him about his parents and the money.

There was no avoiding it any longer. No saying she should come clean with him only to let herself bottle out before it came to actually doing so. This time was it.

'What are you doing tonight?' she blurted out quickly.

'Tonight?' He looked taken aback at her sharp tone.

'I mean, are you on call? Do you need to go into the hospital at all?'

'I wasn't planning on it, no.' He frowned. 'Do you need anything?'

She darted out a tongue to moisten her dry lips.

'I want us to talk. More accurately, there's something I need to tell you…something I should have said a while ago.'

His face closed off, and she could see him mentally withdrawing from her.

'I'm sorry, I've obviously misjudged the situation. We should go back.'

'No, Max.' She reached out, taking his arm and

not letting him pull away from her. 'This is beautiful. Incredible. I'd love to live here with you, and Imogen. Be a proper family.'

His eyes scanned her face as though assessing her sincerity.

'I love you, Max.' The words escaped her lips before she realised it. 'I think I've been falling in love with you ever since I met you.'

There was a fatal beat of silence before he opened his mouth and Evie wished she could take back her involuntary declaration. Not because it wasn't true, but because she was afraid it was too soon for Max.

She didn't want to hear him deny her. Before he could speak, she launched herself forwards, her hands protecting Imogen from being crushed as she planted a kiss on Max's lips.

She'd meant it to silence him, but as he held her in place, deepening the kiss, exploring and teasing, Evie found she couldn't pull away.

Only the ringing of his mobile finally made them reluctantly separate. As he glanced at the screen Max's lips tightened into a thin, disapproving line.

It was irrational, but she couldn't help a shudder of apprehension rippling down her spine.

'I have to take this,' he told her. 'Go inside, look around. I'll catch up with you in a moment.'

Against her better judgement, Evie watched him leave as she continued a tour of the stunning house alone.

She knew the moment he walked into the room that something had changed. That something was very wrong.

'Max...?'

'That was my parents.'

She could actually feel her blood pressure dropping, draining from her head, as her heart slowed down. She reached for the back of a chair to steady herself.

'Your parents? I didn't think...that is...you said you didn't have much contact.'

It wasn't what she meant.

'They were calling to ask me if I'd submitted a medical paper yet on my work in Gaza. I decided it was time they knew about you and Imogen— after all, she is their grandchild. So imagine my surprise when it turns out they already knew all about you both.'

'I wanted to tell you myself—' Evie stumbled but Max interrupted.

'Did my parents *pay* you to keep Imogen a secret from me?'

Quiet fury radiated out of every fibre of him.

She should have told him everything from the

very start, instead of bottling out every time she came close.

'Whatever you think, it isn't like that.'

It sounded clichéd and hollow, but it was the best she had.

The flat, emotionless resonance of his words had cut into her. Whatever she said, it wasn't going to make a difference. An overwhelming sadness consumed her. A sense of grief for what might have been, and the pain of losing yet another person she loved—except this time, it was all her own fault.

'Did you cash their cheque?'

He didn't even realise he'd been holding his breath, fervently urging her to deny it, until she offered a short, jerky nod.

Dammit, he was such a fool.

His whole life he'd looked down on people who believed in love, in others actually loving each other, caring for each other, wanting the best for each other. When he was a child, his parents had mentally knocked any such foolishly romantic notions out of him.

A few minutes ago Evie had promised him that she loved him. Yet lying to him was how she defined love? His response had been on his lips when she'd landed that kiss on his mouth and effectively silenced him. Thank goodness he hadn't told her he loved her in return.

He'd learned to trust himself and his career. Nothing more, nothing less.

And then Evie had come along and shattered all the fortifications he'd built around himself, like a sledgehammer to a landmine.

He had trusted in her. Believed in her. He'd even begun to rewrite his future, a family life with Evie and the beautiful daughter they'd somehow managed to create in that wild week together.

Never once had he thought he could be hurt—no, *wounded*—as deeply as he felt in this moment.

'Please, Max, you have to understand…'

She tailed off on a hopeless cry. He wanted to walk away. He wanted to shut down whatever apology or explanation she was about to offer, but he couldn't. So help him, his feet refused to move.

'All this time, I thought you kept Imogen from me because you felt you would be better off without me. I never once thought it was because you felt you were better off with my parents' money.'

She winced as though the accusation actually hurt her physically, but Max didn't care. He felt too raw, too angry.

'It wasn't like that.'

'Then how was it, Evangeline?' He managed to keep his voice level. He didn't know how.

She started to speak then stopped, shaking her head. The taste of acrid disappointment filled his mouth.

'So it *was* like that,' he bit out in disgust. Though whether more with her, or with himself, he couldn't be sure.

His legs finally began to work again and he turned for the door.

'*No.* No, it wasn't,' she exclaimed. 'Wait, Max, please. I'll…I'll explain everything.'

'I don't want to hear it.'

'Then for Imogen's sake. Please.'

He whirled around, enraged.

'Don't ever, *ever* use our daughter like that again.'

'I'm sorry. You're right.' She stared at him, wild-eyed and teary. 'I don't know why I said that. But I *can* explain. Please.'

He should keep moving. Leave. Every fibre screamed at him to do so.

'You have five minutes,' he ground out.

She nodded, still staring at him in silence.

'Four minutes, forty-five seconds.'

'I wrote you a letter when I first found out I was pregnant,' she blurted out.

'I didn't get it.'

'No. Your parents turned up at Annie's house instead.'

Max glowered, trying to work out whether she was lying or not.

'How would they have known?'

'I didn't know how to contact you out there, and I didn't want a letter like that sitting on your door-mat for months, so I went to HR and got your emergency contact details.'

'And my parents' address,' he realized, raking his hand through his hair. 'Why didn't you just send it to the charity to forward on to me?'

Evie looked aghast.

'I never thought of that.'

And so she'd trusted that his parents would pass the letter on. But they never had.

The truth hit him again and a fresh wave of nausea bubbled in his gut.

'What did your letter say?'

'It…explained how I first found out I was going into first stages of renal failure when I came to Silvertrees. The week we first slept together. Then, a month or so later, I found out I was pregnant.'

'So they read your letter to me, and visited you at your brother's house?' he reminded her flatly.

'Yes,' Evie answered after a moment. 'They accused me of deliberately setting out to trap you.'

Just as he had. The irony wasn't lost on him. His parents were undoubtedly the people he least wanted to emulate and yet here he was, more like them than he had ever realised. It didn't make him feel any better about himself.

But neither did it change the fact that Evie had betrayed him. Lied to him.

'And what did they say?' he asked grimly, not wanting to ask but needing to know their response.

'They told me that losing the baby would be for the best.' Evie gulped, clearly struggling to contain her emotions. 'They told me that if the baby did survive, given that we knew my PKD had developed into kidney failure by that point, the chances of him or her being completely healthy were slim. They also said that you were a successful surgeon with a promising career and they weren't going to let me ruin it.'

A firewall of fury swept through Max. No one should ever treat anyone in that way, least of all someone as kind and giving as Evie. He knew his parents were callous, but even he wouldn't have believed they could stoop so low.

And any promising career only reflected well on

them, Max knew. Their consideration had nothing to do with him, only with themselves.

As Evie hiccupped beside him, he realised she was still fighting to compose herself.

'They told me you weren't interested in a family—which I already knew—but that you would feel obligated to *do the right thing.*'

That brought Max up short. Obligation had definitely been his motivation in the very beginning, but that had quickly, subtly—so subtly he hadn't even noticed it at first—changed. Now he missed both Evie and Imogen when they weren't around, and actively looked forward to going home to them.

Or at least, he had done, until that phone call had turned everything on its head.

Now he felt used, unwanted, a means to an end.

Just as his parents had made him feel as a kid.

'I once told you the one thing I couldn't accept was people making decisions which impacted on me, without even consulting me about it,' he snarled.

'I know. But they told me you would end up resenting me for curtailing your career and ruining your future. More importantly that you would end up resenting Imogen for it.' Evie gave a helpless shrug. 'I could never put my daughter in that position.'

'So you took the money,' he surmised curtly.

'No. Not then. I told them I didn't need their money. I'd stay away if it was for the best, but I wouldn't be bribed to do so. I even ripped the cheque up in front of them.'

Max frowned. He hadn't been told this.

'They said you took the money. *You* even just told me you cashed the cheque.'

She took another deep breath, her hair bouncing around her face as she nodded again.

'When Imogen was born, once I knew she was stable and going to make it, I realised I had to tell you. I wanted to tell you I'd understand if you didn't want to be a part of her life, but I felt you had a right to make that choice.'

'So what changed?'

'Your parents came to me first.'

'My parents did?' He could scarcely believe what she was telling him.

'They'd obviously been monitoring my progress because Imogen was delivered in the afternoon and they got there that night, after visiting hours.'

Max grimaced. He'd always known his parents were emotionally lacking, acting logically and practically, if that seemed somewhat cold to those around them. He could imagine they would have kept an eye on Evie once they'd known about the baby. Not because they were the grandparents— that would have been an emotional connection, which simply wouldn't have occurred to them— but because they would have seen it as their duty. An unwanted obligation.

'I was still groggy, and in shock. I wasn't thinking straight. But then I think a part of me hoped they'd come around, that they'd actually come to see their beautiful granddaughter.'

'It wouldn't have made a difference.' He gritted his teeth.

'No, it didn't,' Evie acknowledged sadly. 'They told me a family was the last thing you needed. And the last thing the baby and I would ultimately want. That we'd end up making each other feel trapped and miserable and that taking the money for my baby would be best for all of us, in the long term. They sounded so convincing.'

'Because that's truly what they would have believed.' Max knitted his brows together, not sure how to explain it to someone who had grown up in such a loving, close-knit family unit.

'They were so...calculated.' She stopped abruptly. 'Sorry.'

'I told you, they don't consult anyone else, they

would have simply decided what *they* felt was in everyone's best interests and then acted accordingly,' he said flatly. 'They will never be able to understand the indescribable pleasure I get from my daughter. Before I met Imogen, even *I* thought being a surgeon would always be the most important thing in my life but I was owed the right to make my own choices. *You* owed me that much.'

'And you blame me for denying you that choice?'

'Yes,' he hissed. 'You kept my daughter from me. You kept your kidney condition from me. You listened to me telling you about my childhood and the way I instigated fights just so that I had a label for the pain I was feeling growing up. And still you never said a word.'

'Because I was frightened, Max.'

'That's it? Fear is your excuse for every decision you made?'

'Yes, because I *was* frightened for my own future health and I was frightened for Imogen's. I was frightened, I was desperate and I was exhausted. The dialysis had taken it out of me and I was staring mortality in the face whilst a tiny, helpless baby was relying on me to get her through her own life. I took the money because I knew it would provide for her if anything happened to me.'

She took a faltering step towards him, her hands

outstretched before checking herself. 'I never touched a penny of it, though. You have to believe that, Max. I set up a proper trust for Imogen. It's all her money. It always would have been.'

'I believe you,' he bit out, the closest he could get to reassuring her.

The fact was, it didn't even matter any more.

The white-hot anger that had initially coursed through him was already beginning to recede. It wasn't about the cheque any more. It wasn't about the money at all. Part of him even felt for Evie, how his parents' reaction must have looked to her. But he still couldn't forgive her for the fact that she'd lied to him.

She'd made every decision unilaterally, impacting on him without him even knowing about it, let alone having any say. And then she'd listened to him tell her about his childhood, about his parents, about his difficult relationship with them, and yet she'd never uttered a word. She'd known about them, met them for herself, and yet whilst he'd been confiding the secrets he'd never told another living soul she'd still kept such a huge secret from him.

That was why he couldn't forgive her.

Max stood, his back to Evie, unable to move a

muscle. Even his jaw was locked, preventing him from answering.

For years he'd told himself he would never allow anyone to get close enough to hurt him. The way his parents had.

Never letting himself get close to anyone had been the only way Max had known to protect himself, and to protect others. He'd become used to being alone, felt safe and protected with a buffer between himself and any other person. He'd had no reason to doubt that he'd be as cold a spouse and parent as his own parents had been.

And then Evangeline Parker had come along to sneak under his skin, bringing with her the most precious gift he had never imagined, in Imogen. He'd let her in, trusted her, been prepared to change his life for her. And now he felt more alone than he had in his life.

'You have to understand why I took the money, Max.' Evie's quietly distraught voice dragged him back to the present.

Even the tears shining in rivers down her cheeks didn't touch him now. He couldn't afford to let them.

'Believe it or not, I *do* understand why,' Max grated out. The anger was receding now, leaving him with a dull ache.

And a void.

'Then we can work through this?' she breathed hopefully.

He shook his head.

'I'm here for Imogen. I'll always be here for her—she's my daughter. But as for you and I, there is no longer any *we*.'

'You just said you understood.' She choked back a sob, and he could see her struggle to stay in control, refusing to break down in front of him.

Part of him could even admire her for it. A lesser woman might have cried and yelled and begged.

'I understand you were frightened for your future. You had no idea if the transplant would be successful and you wanted to secure our daughter's future in the event that you weren't able to pull through.'

'And I didn't know you well enough. When your parents told me you wouldn't want to know about a child, I had no reason to distrust them.'

'I understand that, too. We had a week-long fling. Neither of us had any idea that Imogen would be the result of it.'

Evie bobbed her head, her hair bouncing wildly in her confusion.

'So you understand why I did it, even if I didn't go about it the right way?'

'Yes. But what I don't understand—what I can't forgive—is that you continued to keep it from me.'

'I was scared. I'm sorry,' Evie cried. 'I *wanted* to tell you. I tried so many times. But it never seemed like the right time.'

'It would never have been the *right* time, Evie. But the closest *right* time would have been when I found out I had a daughter you'd been keeping from me. Or when I asked you and Imogen to move in with me here. Or when I told you everything my parents put me through as a kid.'

'Stop. Please.' Evie held up her hand, a distraught expression clouding her features. 'You're right and I'm so, so sorry I never said anything then.'

'What I can't accept is that you probably never would have told me.'

'I would have. Somehow.' She shook her head in despair. 'I was intending to tonight. Remember?'

Yes, he remembered. But that didn't mean anything.

He'd been ready to marry Evie. To make them a proper family, once and for all. Now it was all lost.

He turned for the door.

'I'm going into the hospital after all. I'll drop

you off at the house and I'll leave straight from there.'

'Please, Max. Can't we just talk about this?'

'I don't want to waste my time. Or yours. And I don't want to risk saying something that either of us will regret.'

'When will you be back?'

'In a few days.' That should give him enough time to think.

'Fine,' she said dully. 'Then we'll be gone by the time you get back.'

Max sucked in a breath and turned around.

'Gone?'

'If you can't forgive me, then it's the best thing, isn't it?'

The last scars of his childhood, which had taken so long to heal but had finally knitted over, were ripped open by Evie's words. He would never heal the same way again. He wanted to tell her *no*, that he wasn't ready for that. But she was right, it was the only way, and he had to find a way to move past this in order to have a future with his daughter.

'The best thing. We will need to discuss custody of Imogen, too,' he bit out. 'Shared custody. I won't be just a weekend father to her, Evie.'

'Fine.' There was a desolation in that single syllable that cracked his heart. 'Then I won't be there by the time you get home.'

Max gave a curt nod, unable to speak.

Home? That house would never feel like a home to him again.

CHAPTER FOURTEEN

'IT'S HEALING NICELY.' Max inspected Sally's new graft. It was good work, maybe some of his best yet. The scars would always be there, but they were no longer the marks of her self-harming years. People wouldn't look at her and judge her, condemn her.

'What's happened between you and the doc— why is she back staying with Annie, not you?' Sally cut across him. 'I saw her before she left and she looked worse than she ever did, even with her kidney and the baby, and that's saying something.'

'It's private.' Max glared at the young woman. The last thing he wanted to do was rake over the crippling pain he'd been fighting against ever since Evie and Imogen had left.

'Which means you're trying to pretend everything's okay.'

Nothing was okay. But this wasn't a conversation he wanted to have, even if he was getting the impression Sally didn't care what *he* wanted. His heart plummeted into his new black trainers. Everything was new since Evie and Imogen had gone. Too many memories.

Sally pressed on regardless. 'I think you ought to cut Evie some slack.'

'She told you that, did she? Shouldn't surprise me.'

'No.' The woman clicked her tongue disapprovingly. 'Of course she didn't. She won't tell anyone a thing. But I know, whatever it is, she's blaming herself entirely.'

Despite everything a shaft of pain lanced through him. Evie had already been through more than most people would ever have to endure. He couldn't do anything about the failed situation between the two of them, she had hurt him more than he'd ever thought possible, but that didn't mean he wished any more grief on Evie.

'Well, then, there's no more to say.' Max tried to shut the conversation down but Sally wasn't so easily deterred.

'There is more to say. I'm guessing that, whatever it is, it's something to do with that baby of yours. And the doc loves that little girl with all her heart. Whatever she did, she'll have done with her child's best interests at heart.'

'Sally—' Max began warningly. He might have

known someone who'd been through all this young woman had wasn't about to be intimidated.

'I can see that you're a posh boy, from a good family. I bet you've got parents who would have done anything for you. So isn't it a good thing that Evie's willing to fight for her daughter so that she gets the same chance in life to end up like her doctor mum or surgeon dad? And not someone who didn't have anyone wanting or fighting for them and ends up like me?'

'You had Evie fighting for you. And look at what you've managed to achieve for yourself,' Max answered before his brain could kick into gear.

He didn't need to see the smug look on Sally's face to know he'd just stepped right into her cleverly laid trap.

'See, deep down you really *do* know that the doc's one of the good guys. And when I didn't give you the chance to second-guess yourself, your instinct made you stand up for her.'

Max opened his mouth, wanting to tell Sally it was none of her business. Ironic that she should be so perceptive in how he felt about Evie, yet so wrong about his childhood being so different from her own. But he stopped.

She was right about one thing. It was better that Imogen had someone like Evie, who showered her with love and affection every single day, and was willing to risk everything to protect her. Two things. He *had* instinctively thought well of Evie.

When it came down to a straight choice between him and her daughter, Evie had protected Imogen. Her baby would always come first. Just as he now knew he would put Imogen first if it came down to a choice between his career, and his daughter.

But that didn't stop it from being painful thinking about the way Evie had hurt him.

Although, thanks to Sally's interference, he was starting to wonder if he was looking at it all wrong.

'Thank you, Sally. Most enlightening,' he managed dryly, before stepping around her to open his consulting-room door. 'Now, if you don't have any more questions about your own post-op progress, I'll see you at your next appointment.'

'Fine.' Sally clicked her tongue again. 'Just think about it, okay? I think you and the doc made a great couple. And I don't like to see her so miserable.'

'Goodbye, Sally,' Max said firmly, ushering her out and closing the door behind her with relief. But the thoughts still crowded into his head, as if Sally had jimmied the floodgates open and now he couldn't secure them back again.

When it was time to scrub in for his next surgery,

he'd never felt so relieved. He desperately needed something else on which to focus all his energy.

He was a first-class jackass.

It was Max's first thought as he walked out of the OR to scrub out several hours later. The operation had gone better than he could have planned, yet the only thing on his mind was getting out of here, climbing into his car and going to win Evie back.

Sally was right, even though she didn't know it.

He'd been prepared to forgive his parents for the way they had approached Evie because they assumed he was like them—that his career would be more important to him than his daughter ever could.

They couldn't have been more wrong, and yet he was prepared to forgive them.

Yet Evie, who had tried to protect her own daughter in exactly the same way, was bearing the brunt of his anger. Because he loved her, and so she had an ability to hurt him far more than anyone else ever would.

He was punishing her for being the kind of mother, the kind of partner, he most wanted her to be. The kind who was passionate about those she cared for, and wasn't afraid to show it.

Now he had to show her that he could be the

same way. Because Evie—and indeed Imogen—were integral to his happiness, and it was time to bring them home. If they'd let him.

Grabbing the quickest shower of his life, Max dressed and headed to his office.

His phone rang as he slung his bag over his shoulder and headed for his car, but he ignored it. It didn't matter who it was, he couldn't afford to be distracted. All that mattered was getting to Evie, as fast and as safely as he possibly could.

It was only when he was outside Annie's house, plunged into pitch-blackness, when he retrieved his phone to call Evie and find out just where she was, that he saw the missed call was from Annie.

With uncharacteristically shaky hands, he punched the redial button and waited for the call to pick up.

As he listened to the calm but concise voice on the other end, he felt his whole world fall apart.

'I only saw Evie a few days ago, how can she be showing signs of B-cell rejection?'

Evie heard his voice, thick with emotion, through Annie's speakerphone.

'How can she be showing signs of B-cell rejection?'

Evie shifted in the hospital chair, trying not to

let herself react to the tone of his voice. His evident concern was heartening but it was only natural given how much he had grown to care for his daughter and therefore, by extension, Evie as Imogen's mother. Such concern didn't mean he forgave her, or that he loved her.

'Overnight she started coming down with flu-like symptoms, aching around the kidney site, and she had increased urine output.'

Evie heard Annie try to deliver the information in as clipped a tone as she could over the phone, trying to control her emotions in order to stay businesslike. It was so un-Annie-like that Evie couldn't help a weak smile of affection at the effort her sister-in-law was trying to go to, just to keep Max informed without asking the question she was clearly dying to ask.

Are you going to come down and see her?

A part of Evie longed to ask the same question herself, but she knew what Max's answer would be and she didn't think she could take another rejection.

'Do they know for sure it's rejection?' he demanded sharply over the speakerphone.

'They performed some tests and the creatinine test showed rejection was likely so they've performed a core biopsy.'

'Is she on bed rest in the outpatients whilst they wait for the results?'

'Yes.'

'And if it's confirmed, what's the procedure?'

'What?'

'Annie,' Max snapped, his voice cracking over the line, 'if they determine that it *is* rejection, what will they opt for? Additional plasmapheresis and IVIG sessions?'

'I'm not sure.' Annie glanced desperately at her.

Evie clenched her hands around the covers, trying to calm the lurch of her heart that Max should sound so frantic and *un-surgeon-like*. Almost like any other relative of a patient, concerned for their loved one.

She shook her head. *Now she was just being foolish.*

'No,' Annie said as Evie realised her sister-in-law had mistaken her headshake for rebuttal.

'Sorry, sorry,' Evie cried. 'Yes, they'll probably look at additional plasmapheresis and IVIG as a first port of call.'

'Evie?' Max's voice reverberated around the room. 'Can you hear me? Just hold on, I'm going to end this call so I can phone your Transfer team down there and get some more information. Okay?'

Evie couldn't meet Annie's gaze as she tried not

to let her emotions show, but she was sure the whole hospital could hear her heart hammering a military drum tattoo inside her chest.

Was that professional concern? Concern for the mother of his daughter? Or, could it be possible, genuine concern for the woman he'd realised he loved? And this time, when she tried to reprimand herself that she was being unrealistic, the spark of hope refused to be stamped out.

'All right,' Annie was saying. 'Shall I...? Do you want me to call you with updates?'

'Sorry?'

So she'd got it all wrong.

His surprise at why he should need to be kept informed was a kick in the teeth. Evie tried but she couldn't stop the tears of regret from welling in her eyes. Even Annie's tone changed as she turned her back to speak quickly and quietly into the phone.

'To let you know how Evie is doing? She told me not to bother you, after your conversation the other day. But then we agreed it was better to tell you so that you could decide whether you wanted to come down for your daughter or whether you were happy for my husband and me to look after Imogen.'

'Ah, right.' He sounded genuinely sorry he'd misunderstood, at least. 'Actually, Annie, I think it's probably better for Imogen to stay in a constant environment with your family rather than be pulled from pillar to post coming back up to me whilst Evie is down there.'

A fresh wave of nausea rolled over Evie. It was enough that he couldn't forgive her, but she didn't want to be the cause of a rift in his new relationship with his daughter.

'Fine,' she heard Annie respond flatly, but her irritation with Max was audible. 'Then the baby will stay with us. We'd love to have her longer. Just thought you might, too.'

'Okay. Tell Evie it's going to be fine.'

Evie stared across the room in shock. Max never said that. He never promised anyone everything would be fine. *Never.*

'And tell her I'll be with her in...'

The line crackled as he faded out but it sounded as if he'd said *half an hour.* That couldn't be right.

'What?' Annie's shock was nothing compared to the way Evie's heart leaped. 'I can't hear you clearly.'

Still, that couldn't be right—it was a much longer drive than that.

'Sorry, heading into a tunnel so I'll probably get cut off any minute. I said I should be there in half an hour.'

'How?' Annie voiced Evie's thoughts, but the line cracked again and went dead.

Evie stared at her sister-in-law in disbelief before a heavy tear trickled down one cheek. Hope, confusion, anticipation, expectation—it was all in that one salty droplet.

'Did he mean the Meadowall Tunnel between my house and here?' Annie asked slowly.

Leaning her head back on the pillows, Evie just shook her head and hoped.

'Feeling pretty bad?' The gruff voice woke Evie from her fitful slumber and she snapped her head up in disbelief. She hardly dared to open her eyes too quickly in case she found he wasn't really there.

Nope. He was reassuringly solid.

She drank in the sight, but slowly the dark-circled eyes, unshaven stubble, and slightly haunted expression registered. It gave her something to cling to.

'I'm about as good as you look,' she murmured shakily.

'That bad, huh?' His eyes were loaded with regret.

'Pretty much. I can't believe I fell asleep. When did Annie go?'

'You're exhausted. Annie said you dozed off as

soon as our phone call ended and she stayed with you until I got here.'

'Half an hour?'

'Twenty-four minutes.'

'You really were already down here?' A few more restraints of caution gave way.

'Outside Annie's house,' he confirmed quietly.

He stepped towards her and she offered no resistance as he snaked his arms around her shoulders and drew her in. Instead, Evie closed her eyes and allowed his familiar citrusy, musky, masculine scent fill her senses. Max dropped a kiss on her head.

Still they didn't speak.

Beyond her, the rest of the hospital fell away. Just like the first time, it was just her and him, and nothing else.

'Why are you here, Max?' she mumbled against the rock wall of his chest.

'To bring you home.' His words were muffled, spoken into her hair. She had a feeling he was breathing her in just as she'd done with him. Her heart cracked.

'What's changed?'

He paused a bit before saying the word she didn't want to hear.

'Nothing. Everything.'

'Max...' She drew her head back but didn't pull away. 'I *am* sorry.'

He shushed her.

'No, it's my turn now. I should have accepted your apology that afternoon, but I was being pig-headed. I know you were scared to tell me, and that you couldn't have been sure what my reaction would have been. Just because I know what my parents are like doesn't mean you did.'

'What about betraying your trust? You said you couldn't forgive me.'

'I was being an idiot. I'm sorry. I was thinking of my own feelings where you were more concerned about our daughter. That won't happen from here on.'

'From here on?' Evie whispered, needing to hear Max say the words. 'Does that mean you want Imogen and me to come back with you?'

'No.'

She tipped her head back, confused.

'You said before that you wanted to bring Imogen and I home.'

'Yes, but not my old place—why should you two have to move? I'll move down here and we'll get a new place. A home of our own.'

'You're leaving Silvertrees?'

She should be more circumspect but she couldn't

stop a tiny balloon of elation floating up inside her, lifting some of the darkest fears about this recent rejection episode.

'You said to me a month ago that this is where you love to be.' Max nodded. 'Your family is here, you and Imogen have ties here. I don't have ties up there. It's just a job. I can find a job anywhere. So we find a house you love near your brother and Annie, and we start a new life together as a proper family.'

'But you still intend that I should give up my career?'

'Actually, no. Sally told me about a centre she visits down here, with a whole new set of kids just desperate for someone like you to believe in them, fight for them. I spoke to one of the board members on the drive down. We need a proper meeting to hammer out the details but they've been hoping to approach you for quite a while. They also know of me by reputation and would be more than happy to welcome me as their new go-to paediatric plastic surgeon.'

'Working together?' She couldn't seem to process what he was telling her.

'Side by side, whenever you needed me.'

It all sounded too good to be true. And yet it was

true. Max was here, and he was offering all she'd ever wanted. And more.

'You would do that for me? For Imogen?'

'I would. And for me. I realised that I don't give half as much back as you do, and it's time I started.'

'You've got it all figured out, haven't you?' Evie marvelled.

'Pretty much. There's just one thing left.'

She didn't realise what he was doing until she felt the cool metal sliding over her finger. The ring was stunning, a classic grain-cut solitaire diamond ring set in a platinum band with alternate diamonds and rubies set into each shoulder.

'I never make promises I can't keep. So believe me when I promise I'll love you until the day I die. Marry me, Evie?'

Looking up into his face, she realised how real it was. No more secrets, No more lies. Just the promise of love and support and a future with the man she loved.

A long, long future. She was determined of that.

'Yes,' she whispered with a throaty chuckle, unable to resist teasing him. 'And I promise to love you until the day *you* die, too.'

'Minx.' He grinned against her lips as he slid his hands into her hair to draw her into an intense, toe-curling kiss.

EPILOGUE

'NICE MEDAL. SNAP!' Max teased as Evie ran towards him, brandishing her newest necklace and with her space blanket billowing out behind her like a cape.

'His and hers?' She arched her eyebrows in amusement.

'Quite.' He laughed. 'You looked fantastic coming over that finishing line, by the way.'

'Thanks, I was just glad the whole thing was over. I don't think I could have raced another metre. But this finishers' medal makes it all worthwhile, even if I am somewhere around five hundredth according to the race officials.'

'Yeah, well, never mind the four hundred and ninety-nine. How many of them are former transplant recipients?' Max snorted dismissively. He was immensely proud of his wife and, judging by the beam on her face, she felt just as proud of herself. 'Besides, I heard that over one thousand competitors started this year, so you've beaten over half of them.'

'True,' chuckled Evie. 'So, I got Annie's right kidney round a half-mile swim, a seventeen-mile bike ride and a five-mile run in one hour and fifty-nine minutes. How's her left kidney doing?'

'This is your first triathlon, ever, and still you're so damn competitive.' He dropped a kiss on her nose.

'Mmm-hmm. It's also my transplant's five-year anniversary, with no rejection episodes since that initial blip.' She snuggled against his chest before pulling her head back excitedly. 'I'm feeling in-credible. So, about Annie's other kidney?'

'I actually don't know, sorry,' he relented. 'I haven't seen your brother since the last change-over points where he was waiting for Annie, but I think he said she was about fifteen minutes be-hind you at that point, and you know you're a faster runner than she is.'

'She'll probably be coming in between two hours twenty and two hours thirty, then.' Evie glanced at her watch. 'Shall we head back to the finish line?'

'Good idea. I said we'd meet everyone there so look out for Imogen—she's probably still com-mandeering your brother's shoulders for the best view in the house.'

'She would. She's the cheekiest five-and-a-half-year-old I've ever known.' Evie clicked her tongue but Max wasn't fooled; her love for their two children radiated through everything she did. 'What about Toby?'

'He's doing what he always does in the middle of the afternoon...'

'Sleeping,' she chimed in, laughing. 'I bet my brother's pushed him the whole way around in that off-road racer pram you bought.'

'You can count on it.'

They jostled their way good-humouredly against the finishers coming towards them, finally making it back to the finish line to look out for their family.

It felt good to Max.

The last five years had been the best of his life since he'd left Silvertrees to move to within fifteen minutes of Evie's family. Unexpectedly, he'd not only gained a family in Evie and Imogen, but he'd also gained the family he'd never had in Annie's family, too.

The ink had barely been dry on his resignation when the job offers had flooded in, and he had happily accepted a generous promotion package to the top local hospital, which had included a relocation incentive to the house of their dreams. But, more importantly, they had accepted his proviso that he must also have time to work with some of the troubled teens from the new centre where Evie had returned to part-time work along with having time with her family.

The fact that they were doing this race today for Sally seemed so perfectly fitting. Free of the recognisable silvery lines, Sally had easily found her dream job, which had previously eluded her, and it had also given her the confidence to start charity work in her spare time for the residential centre where she'd first met Evie.

Max wrapped his arms around his wife feeling, as he did every day, contented and relaxed.

'Do you know, between you, Annie and I, we've raised money well into five figures?' he murmured into her ear, revelling in the look of proud shock as she twisted her head to look up at him.

'Seriously? That's incredible. Does Sally know? She'll be over the moon.'

'Sally's the one who told me.' Max nibbled Evie's ear, causing her to inadvertently wiggle against him.

'What about you, anyway? How did you do?'

'I didn't do too badly.'

She pulled out of his arms and spun around.

'You didn't win, did you?'

'Who do you think I am? Superman? No, I didn't win.'

She poked him playfully in the ribs.

'What was your time, then?'

He grinned until she shrieked with anticipation.

'Oh, come on, Max, you have to tell me.'

'One hour, twenty-seven minutes.'

'Wow...' She soberly bestowed a kiss on his lips. 'That *has* to be a high position?'

'Within the top ten.'

'That seriously deserves a prize.' She adopted a serious expression. 'I feel I should reward you.'

'Oh, really?' He pulled her to him, the crowd surging unconcerned around them.

'Yes, really. Tonight,' she clarified, snaking her arms around him. 'When we're alone.'

'I think I love the idea but I have a feeling that you might be too tired for anything tonight.' He smiled, lowering his mouth to drop a soft kiss on her lips, surprised when she deepened it to something full of promise.

'It's funny,' she whispered, 'but suddenly I find I have untapped resources of energy these days. Must have been the white chocolate and raspberry muffin you gave me this morning before the race, but I feel there's nothing I can't handle.'

'That,' he murmured gently, kissing his wife again, 'I don't doubt.'

* * * * *

If you enjoyed this story, check out the great debut from Charlotte Hawkes

THE ARMY DOC'S SECRET WIFE

Available now!

MILLS & BOON®
Large Print Medical

August

Their Meant-to-Be Baby	Caroline Anderson
A Mummy for His Baby	Molly Evans
Rafael's One Night Bombshell	Tina Beckett
Dante's Shock Proposal	Amalie Berlin
A Forever Family for the Army Doc	Meredith Webber
The Nurse and the Single Dad	Dianne Drake

September

Their Secret Royal Baby	Carol Marinelli
Her Hot Highland Doc	Annie O'Neil
His Pregnant Royal Bride	Amy Ruttan
Baby Surprise for the Doctor Prince	Robin Gianna
Resisting Her Army Doc Rival	Sue MacKay
A Month to Marry the Midwife	Fiona McArthur

October

Their One Night Baby	Carol Marinelli
Forbidden to the Playboy Surgeon	Fiona Lowe
A Mother to Make a Family	Emily Forbes
The Nurse's Baby Secret	Janice Lynn
The Boss Who Stole Her Heart	Jennifer Taylor
Reunited by Their Pregnancy Surprise	Louisa Heaton

MILLS & BOON®
Large Print Medical

November

Mummy, Nurse...Duchess?	Kate Hardy
Falling for the Foster Mum	Karin Baine
The Doctor and the Princess	Scarlet Wilson
Miracle for the Neurosurgeon	Lynne Marshall
English Rose for the Sicilian Doc	Annie Claydon
Engaged to the Doctor Sheikh	Meredith Webber

December

Healing the Sheikh's Heart	Annie O'Neil
A Life-Saving Reunion	Alison Roberts
The Surgeon's Cinderella	Susan Carlisle
Saved by Doctor Dreamy	Dianne Drake
Pregnant with the Boss's Baby	Sue MacKay
Reunited with His Runaway Doc	Lucy Clark

January

The Surrogate's Unexpected Miracle	Alison Roberts
Convenient Marriage, Surprise Twins	Amy Ruttan
The Doctor's Secret Son	Janice Lynn
Reforming the Playboy	Karin Baine
Their Double Baby Gift	Louisa Heaton
Saving Baby Amy	Annie Claydon

MILLS & BOON®
Large Print – August 2017

ROMANCE

The Italian's One-Night Baby	Lynne Graham
The Desert King's Captive Bride	Annie West
Once a Moretti Wife	Michelle Smart
The Boss's Nine-Month Negotiation	Maya Blake
The Secret Heir of Alazar	Kate Hewitt
Crowned for the Drakon Legacy	Tara Pammi
His Mistress with Two Secrets	Dani Collins
Stranded with the Secret Billionaire	Marion Lennox
Reunited by a Baby Bombshell	Barbara Hannay
The Spanish Tycoon's Takeover	Michelle Douglas
Miss Prim and the Maverick Millionaire	Nina Singh

HISTORICAL

Claiming His Desert Princess	Marguerite Kaye
Bound by Their Secret Passion	Diane Gaston
The Wallflower Duchess	Liz Tyner
Captive of the Viking	Juliet Landon
The Spaniard's Innocent Maiden	Greta Gilbert

MEDICAL

Their Meant-to-Be Baby	Caroline Anderson
A Mummy for His Baby	Molly Evans
Rafael's One Night Bombshell	Tina Beckett
Dante's Shock Proposal	Amalie Berlin
A Forever Family for the Army Doc	Meredith Webber
The Nurse and the Single Dad	Dianne Drake

0717 GEN STD LP

MILLS & BOON®

Why shop at millsandboon.co.uk?

Each year, thousands of romance readers find their perfect read at millsandboon.co.uk. That's because we're passionate about bringing you the very best romantic fiction. Here are some of the advantages of shopping at www.millsandboon.co.uk:

* **Get new books first**—you'll be able to buy your favourite books one month before they hit the shops

* **Get exclusive discounts**—you'll also be able to buy our specially created monthly collections, with up to 50% off the RRP

* **Find your favourite authors**—latest news, interviews and new releases for all your favourite authors and series on our website, plus ideas for what to try next

* **Join in**—once you've bought your favourite books, don't forget to register with us to rate, review and join in the discussions

Visit **www.millsandboon.co.uk**
for all this and more today!